Burn The Evidence

Detective Solomon Gray, Volume 2

Keith Nixon

Published by Gladius Press, 2019.

Burn The Evidence
A Solomon Gray Novel
Keith Nixon

One

Rachel lay in bed, staring at a ceiling she couldn't see in the darkness. Her brother, Jonathan, was a few feet away; his breathing, regular and deep.

The problem was her father. Or at least it could be, Rachel wasn't sure. His place was in a cot bed on the other side of the room, next to the door. Trouble was, she was unable to tell if he was asleep or just pretending, trying to catch her out.

The holiday – only a few short days – was over already. In the morning, they'd be heading back to smoggy London, a million miles away from Margate. A million miles from Cameron. She simply had to see Cameron one last time before she left, no matter what her father thought.

Rachel pushed back the covers, put her feet onto the carpeted floor, the thick pile pushing between her toes, and carefully got up. The bed creaked. She froze. Jonathan stirred, rolled over. Nothing from her father. She dressed quietly, pulling on a pair of trousers and slipping a top over her vest. She picked up her shoes; didn't bother putting them on, she'd do so downstairs.

She crept across the room, avoiding the squeaky floorboard. She almost made it. The door was half open when her father said, "Going somewhere, Rach?"

Over her shoulder she could see him sitting up in bed, silhouetted by the weak light from the landing. He must have been awake all along. "I wanted to watch the waves," she said.

Her father rose and crossed over to her. His expression was a frown, as was the tone of his voice. "Are you going to see ... him?"

"No," she lied once more, hating to do this to her father, but she had to. Love won over everything, didn't it? "Please? Just for a little while."

Her father sighed. Rachel knew then that he'd fold. He'd been easy on her and Jonathan since they'd come back home. After her mother disappeared, leaving Rachel and Jonathan to fend for themselves.

"Come here," said her father, beckoning.

Rachel went to him, leaving the door open behind her. He enveloped her in his strong arms. She smelt his body odour. It wasn't strong or off-putting, just a natural smell. He stepped back, put a hand on her shoulder.

"Go back to bed, Rach," he said.

"What?" Rachel couldn't believe it. She took a step back, shook his hand off, then another step.

"You're too young to be meeting a boy at this time of night."

"I'm sixteen soon. And I love him!"

"You can't possibly know what love is at your age."

The derision was obvious in his voice, it cut through her. Tears in her eyes, she turned and ran out the door, pulling it closed behind her, shoes still in her hands.

"Rachel!" shouted her father.

She barrelled down the stairs, one flight after another. His heavy feet were close behind. He couldn't catch her, not now. When she reached the bottom, the light was on in the hall. Mrs Renishaw, who ran the Sunset guest house, standing in the doorway wearing a dressing gown, her old-fashioned perm in a net.

"What's going on?" she asked.

Rachel didn't pause to answer, but made a dash for the front door. She twisted the Yale lock and was onto the pavement before her father got outside. She heard Mrs Renishaw ask her question again, louder this time. Rachel sprinted, heading down the hill, past the Winter Gardens.

"Rachel!"

She glanced over her shoulder. Her father was standing on the top step; Mrs Renishaw at his elbow, peering past him. He called once more. Rachel ignored him.

An hour, that was all. An hour with Cameron. It wasn't long. It would be over before they knew it. When Rachel got back to the guest house she'd apologise and her father would forgive her. Eventually.

But for now, Cameron was her focus. He'd be waiting for her at the harbour, as they'd arranged.

The trouble was, for Rachel, in that hour everything would change.

Two

Ten Years Later

Solomon Gray dug around in the pouch at his waist and grabbed hold of two cartridges. He slotted them into the cracked open barrel, snapped the weapon shut. He stood with one foot forward and the shotgun only half raised, held away from his chest.

"Pull!"

Gray sighted the clay before he nestled the weapon. It had to be firmly in place, otherwise the kick of the recoil could do serious damage, possibly even dislocate his shoulder. A circle the size of a saucer was fired across Gray, heading from left to right. He tracked the clay and fired, two rapid blasts, one after the other. The clay carried on into the trees, untouched.

"Looks like the drinks are on me tonight," said Gray.

"You're just rusty," said Jeff Carslake.

"It's been a while, right enough."

If Gray remembered correctly, at least six years. He'd sold his gun back then too. He couldn't be bothered with the rigours of maintaining a licence for something he didn't see himself using again, so he was borrowing Carslake's spare. It was heavy, unfamiliar. At first his aim had been surprisingly decent, though the initial targets were the easy ones, fired at a shallow, rising angle. Gray had plenty of time to zero-in on the clay. However, since then the difficulty had increased and

Carslake's more trained eye meant Gray's score had fallen further and further behind his friend's.

"Try again. Think in terms of shooting down a plane."

Gray reloaded. "Pull!" He tracked the gun slightly ahead of the clay and fired. The pellets clipped the edge. It was a hit and therefore a point, but Gray was disappointed. The next he blew apart.

"You're getting the hang of it," said Carslake. He took Gray's position on the shooting platform, nestled the shotgun tight into his shoulder and stared down at the sight. "Pull!"

His shot blasted the circle into smithereens. Gray sighed.

Half an hour later, the course completed, Carslake and Gray were in the bar. Gray carried the drinks over to the corner table where Carslake was seated.

Gray raised his glass in salute to the winner.

Carslake bowed. "It's good doing this again, Sol."

"Yes," agreed Gray. And it was. In fact, Gray felt great. He and Carslake used to come here regularly after work, rather than taking a day off as they had on this occasion. They'd been fiercely competitive, Gray the slightly better of the pair back then. Spending time together outside work socially. Gray with other people. It seemed familiar, yet odd.

"Same time next week? One evening, maybe?"

"Definitely."

"Won't be long before you'll be giving me a run for my money."

"Who knows, I may practise when I'm off-shift."

Carslake laughed. Gray fidgeted; he had a question burning in his mind.

"Did you hear any more from your contact?" asked Gray. "About Tom?"

"As a matter of fact, I did." Carslake put his glass down. "Today, actually."

Gray leaned forward. "Was it him? Was it Tom at the ferry port?"

"Maybe."

"How can it be a 'maybe'? Either it was Tom or it wasn't?"

"A decade's a long time for someone's memory to falter. Christ, a witness can be unreliable within minutes, never mind years! You know that."

Gray rubbed a hand over his face. "Sorry, it's just bloody frustrating."

"Not necessarily."

"Why has all this only just come to light?"

"It seems some case material was lost."

"What material?" Gray went cold, he'd possessed every piece of documentation relating to his son's disappearance and now it appeared the collection had been incomplete. Ten years of searching knocked off track because of a missing piece of paper.

"A witness statement. The man my contact spoke to is retired now but still lives in Dover. He definitely recalled seeing a boy, possibly matching Tom's description, in the back of a car as it was driving onto the ferry. He remembered it because the boy had looked petrified. I drove there myself and showed him Tom's photograph. He's pretty sure it was him. It seems Tom was being taken to France."

"Why didn't you tell me, Jeff?" Gray was stunned by the revelation. "I could have spoken to him myself. He may have given me something vital!" Gray was almost shouting. People in the bar were turning to stare.

"For God's sake, Sol. Keep your voice down."

"I don't give a shit what anyone else here thinks," said Gray, but lowered his tone. "This is my *son* we're talking about."

"Your response is exactly why I kept this from you, Sol. If the lead had come to nothing how would you have felt then?"

Numb, thought Gray. *Like always.* He said, "Where does the witness live? I want to meet him."

"Just outside Dover, in St. Margaret's – and I'll arrange it, of course."

"As soon as you can."

"Of course. Look, Sol. This is a really good development. You should be pleased. It's more than you've had for years."

"Sorry, Jeff. I'm delighted."

"I haven't stopped pursuing this either. The search continues in France. The trouble is, from there he could have been moved anywhere. The haystack just got a lot, lot bigger."

"Thanks, Jeff." He felt guilty now for going off at Carslake.

"No need to thank me. That's what friends are for."

Gray's mobile rang. His hands were shaking with emotion as he pressed the green key. He listened briefly to the caller before disconnecting.

"What?" asked Carslake.

"There's a body on the beach."

Gray's day off was over.

Three

The body lay face down, its weight creating a depression in the wet sand. One brown arm was flung out, the other tucked beneath the torso. Both shoes were missing; bare feet on show. The toes were crushed together, overlapping one another, Gray guessed, from being squeezed into footwear several sizes too small over a long period of time. The clothes were still sodden, the waves breaking a few feet away, the tide retreating.

A runner out in the early morning March sunlight had spotted the body. At that point, the mud-coloured water had only released the upper third of its prize. By the time Detective Sergeant Solomon Gray arrived, all was revealed.

What made the corpse stand out against the dull background was the fluorescent yellow buoyancy aid, straps over the shoulders and a belt tied around the waist. The "life" jacket had proved useless at its one and only task.

Experienced sailors spent good money on reputable brands – the flotation devices literally could be the difference between survival and death. Novices, like weekend kayakers, usually went cheap. Fine if the shore was within spitting distance and the water a millpond.

Further along the shore, stranded on seaweed-strewn chalk and flint rocks, was a deflated dinghy. It lay like a banana skin, discarded, battered, and bruised.

The wind had whipped Gray's clifftop flat last night, stopped him getting to sleep. It had been breezy all day. These days he lived not much more than a mile from here, a stretch of beach about midway between the resorts of Broadstairs and Ramsgate. Gray expected the dinghy had been pitched over by high waves, or had suffered a puncture. Whichever, the end result was a washed-up corpse.

Centuries ago, this area of coastline had been the covert port of entry for contraband smugglers, bringing ashore alcohol and tobacco at an out-of-the-way place to avoid customs tax. The entrances to caves and tunnels, cut into the soft chalk, still existed. These days the illegal "cargo" was people.

The bay could only be reached when the tide was low. After a hike from the nearest break in the cliffs, it was popular with tourists, offering a café and toilets where Gray had descended a footpath. Most people rarely made it this far, choosing to stay close to the amenities, but Gray had walked this route many times on his way to Ramsgate. It was the perfect landing spot if you didn't want to be seen. At night nobody came here.

"Another bloody immigrant." Detective Sergeant Mike Fowler stood beside Gray, a foot shorter in height and broader in the chest; powerfully built. Fowler sported a porn-star moustache — a relic from an annual charity event — and a sneer.

Gray suspected Fowler was right, though silently thought *it's refugee, not immigrant, you idiot*. Incidences of trafficking had soared over the last few years. They were so close to the European continent, France and Belgium could be seen on a clear day.

In times of austerity and high unemployment, people-smuggling was one of the few growth industries; a classic scenario where demand dramatically outstripped supply, where desperation and hope were ruthlessly exploited. Money changed hands, risks were taken, people died.

Still, even if Fowler was probably right, Gray wasn't going to say so.

"Another bloody person, you mean."

Fowler was no more than a colleague to Gray these days, their friendship stretched and strained through years of conflict that just never quite seemed to go away.

"No, I really don't. I mean, who goes out in a dinghy at the dead of night otherwise?"

Gray could see his point, but where were the rest? Trafficked people were always brought ashore in groups.

"Show some compassion, man."

"For what? They're like bugs. One disappears; three more materialise in their place. We're overrun. It can't carry on."

Gray's heartburn flared up again. Periodically, he experienced a discomfort in his chest cavity, a pressure within, often when Fowler was around and his stress levels rose. Usually a drink of milk calmed it, but there was none to hand out here.

"You all right?" asked Fowler.

"Fine, thanks." Gray swallowed repeatedly which helped a little.

"Good, don't want you dying on me. I've enough paperwork to deal with."

Fowler squatted down to get a closer look at the cadaver, habitually stroking his nicotine-stained moustache as he ran his eyes over the man. Fowler wouldn't really be interested in what he saw; it was simply a mechanism to break the conversation. Not that Gray cared. He and Fowler were at opposite ends of the spectrum when it came to immigration. However, xenophobia was like a virus, more and more people catching the disease, openly voicing views similar to Fowler's.

Recently there had been a change in the smugglers' strategies. The obvious tactics, like shoving a group of migrants into the back of a lorry and driving it through a major port, such as Dover or Folkestone, was over. These routes were too well monitored. So, starting a few months ago, the process had shifted to using small boats; ferrying handfuls of refugees at a time onto out-of-the-way beaches. It was impossible for the authorities to patrol everywhere.

Gray knew, because he'd looked it up online via the Ordnance Survey, that the UK mainland coast stretched to over 11,000 miles. An impossible task to keep an eye on every potential landing spot, even before the police force had been hacked back by the Tory government's austerity measures.

But there were easier places to land than Thanet. Like Deal, just along the coast between here and Dover, where there was an extensive stretch of shoreline, miles long, mostly shrouded in darkness, rarely patrolled. And there were no cliffs. It still had a small fishing population, therefore the coming and going of boats at night wasn't going to raise alarm. It was perfect.

"I'm turning him over," said Fowler, seeking permission from Gray as the senior of the pair, yet not. Photographs of the body in situ had already been captured by a Scene of Crime Officer. Fowler took out a pair of nitrile gloves from a pocket and pulled them on before he flipped the corpse.

The dead man's eyes and mouth were open in an apparent scream. Gray had seen enough bodies to know the cause was nothing so melodramatic, simply a slackening of the muscles. He appeared to have Middle Eastern descent, going by his skin colour. The beard was pretty typical too. A search of his pockets by Fowler revealed nothing. He stood, began to say something, but was interrupted.

"Sarge!" A shout from one of the uniforms, jabbing urgently at the diminishing tide line. Gray reacted first, Fowler much slower, far less interested.

A uniform was knee-deep in the surf, holding another corpse; floating, half submerged and face up. He was familiar. Without pause, and careless of a soaking, Gray waded into the sea; his suspicions confirmed as he closed in on the body. He was no immigrant. Gray knew this man and all too well.

"Get him ashore," said Gray. He pulled his mobile out to make a call.

There was trouble ahead.

BY THE TIME DETECTIVE Inspector Yvonne Hamson arrived, the receding tide had released a third corpse. She brought more cops, more Scenes Of Crime Officers, more activity. She had become the Senior Investigating Officer; the case belonged to her now.

Hamson was nearly six foot. In heels she was almost as tall as Gray. Today she wore trainers. Usually, Hamson was elegant, well dressed, aware of her appearance. But pressures in her private life were taking their toll.

As Hamson walked down the beach, Fowler retreated to the foot of the chalk cliffs. Wafts of white clouds showed he was smoking, taking a break. Hamson and Fowler kept their distance from each other, their relationship to colleagues seemingly frosty, the reality anything but. Only Gray knew Fowler and Hamson were having an affair, as Fowler and his wife had split up but weren't yet divorced. It was a secret Gray had to keep because Hamson had confided in him and him alone.

The increased importance of the investigation also brought Brian Blake, the Crime Scene Manager, to the locus. The SOCOs were his to command, and Blake never missed a prominent event.

Hamson turned her back on Fowler and Blake, dismissing them. "Are you sure it's Regan Armitage?"

"He looks a little worse for wear after his immersion, but it's definitely him." The body was battered and bruised, various abrasions on his face, clothes ripped. He lay on his back, eyes closed, mouth open.

"What the hell was he doing out here?"

"Dying, clearly."

"You'll make a fine detective one day."

Regan was the tearaway son of prominent and wealthy local businessman, Jake Armitage, a man who divided opinion. Regan was handsome, aloof, arrogant. Popular with a few, disliked by many, just like his old man. Born into privilege and pre-disposed to make sure everyone knew it. As a kid he'd regularly been in trouble and known to the police. Even now, well into his twenties, he remained a familiar face in the cells.

"What about the other two?" asked Hamson.

"One appears to have drowned, one probably not."

"Why probably not?"

"Best you see."

Gray led Hamson along the shoreline, bypassed one corpse, stopped at the furthest. He crouched down and pointed.

Hamson, bending at the waist, said, "A stab wound. Puts a different complexion on the situation."

"Perhaps they fell out on the final leg, got into a fight, ended up overboard?"

"Maybe."

Blake sauntered over. Crime Scene Manager was a title which aptly fitted his role. An overseer, rather than a do-er. "Delegate" was his middle name. He'd dropped a little weight recently and tidied himself up, but male model he was not.

"We're pretty much done here," said Blake. "Not a lot to reveal." It wasn't surprising that evidence was thin. Water had a cleansing behaviour when it came to crime. There might be value in a fingertip search of the beach above the tideline, though Gray wasn't hopeful.

Hamson nodded sharply, keeping communication to an absolute minimum as usual. Blake, job done, gladly retreated.

Gray shoved his hands into his pockets, raised the obvious point. "Jake Armitage will need to be told."

"I suppose you mean by me." Nobody liked delivering a death knock.

"By us. Jake is old-school arsehole. He's not what you'd call a people person. I'll even drive."

"You're all heart."

"Sure, just don't tell anyone."

"Nobody would believe me anyway. I'd better give Carslake an update." Detective Chief Inspector Jeff Carslake was her immediate boss. Hamson dialled but couldn't get through. She didn't seem particularly bothered. "I'll try again later."

As they began the long trek back to the car, staff from the coroner's office arrived to remove the cadavers in readiness for Ben Clough the pathologist's slice-and-dice post-mortem routine.

Gray would prefer to watch a body being cut up rather than visit Jake Armitage. However, you didn't always get what you wanted.

Four

A woman with a couple of kids hanging off her legs was standing like an edifice on the corner of the concrete esplanade scrutinising Gray and Hamson as they made their way along the beach.

When they reached the top of the slipway the woman spoke.

"Excuse me, are you with this lot?" She pointed to a disorderly array of police cars and Scene of Crime vans, parked in front of a line of beach huts which followed the curvature of the cliff in the space where deck chairs would usually be located.

"Yes," said Hamson.

The woman introduced herself as Mrs Fiona Emerson. She was tall and thin with a pinched face and wore a loose-fitting flowery dress. Her greying hair was tied up, and sunglasses rested on her head just beneath the bun. A short, balding man, wearing, of all things, a knitted tank top, hung back. Far enough away to stay out of it; close enough to react should he be called forward. Gray assumed he was the partner.

"We're investigating a serious incident further down the beach," said Hamson.

"Oh, I couldn't care less about that." Mrs Emerson dismissed someone else's misfortune with an imperious wave. "I rang you people earlier. We've been waiting."

"What about?"

"We were confronted by a man with a knife."

Gray immediately pricked his ears up at this. He glanced at Hamson. By her expression she felt the same interest. The call must have got lost in all the recent activity. "When was this?"

"Less than a quarter of an hour ago. We usually arrive early to get a good space on the sand. I found the locks smashed off our beach hut and a man inside sleeping on the floor." Mrs Emerson pointed towards her hut.

The subject of her concern was a small pile of clothes on the floor. Next to them lay a fluorescent yellow life jacket. It appeared someone had survived the landing.

"Get Blake," said Hamson unnecessarily. Gray was already digging his mobile out of a pocket to place the call to the Crime Scene Manager. While they waited for him to arrive, Hamson took a closer look inside the hut, leaving Gray with Mrs Emerson.

"Originally from London," she said. "Moved to Broadstairs for the quiet life." She delivered the last comment with a distinct tinge of sarcasm, as if the intruder was Gray's fault.

"What did he look like?" asked Gray.

"A foreigner," she shrugged.

Gray waited for more. Mrs Emerson obviously felt as if this was enough of a description. "And?"

"What?"

"Height, skin colour, accent? Anything distinguishing?"

"For God's sake, I don't know! He was just a *man*!"

"Please try and remember. Any detail could help us find him," said Gray.

Mrs Emerson huffed. "Average height, brown skin, dark curly hair, bearded, and aggressive."

"Did he speak?"

"No. He just came at me when I discovered him. I backed away, and he ran past. I told Philip to stop him, but he was useless."

Philip, the partner, scowled at her sleight, though held his tongue. Gray didn't blame him for not tackling a knife-wielding stranger, but clearly his wife did. Blake's arrival saved Gray from making any comment.

"What have we got here then?" asked the Crime Scene Manager. Gray explained the situation while a SOCO cordoned off the hut and got to work.

Blake was clearly unnerved by the hovering Mrs Emerson, who wanted her space back as quickly as possible. So much so he quickly cleared out of her hut, leaving one of his men to the inspection process; lifting fingerprints, bagging the clothes and life jacket.

"I feel sorry for the husband," said Blake who was keeping Gray between him and Mrs Emerson. Hamson had made herself scarce to call Carslake again.

"Usually people get the partner they deserve," said Gray.

Gray remained implacable under Blake's stare.

"Anything?" asked Gray.

"Lots of prints. The small ones are easy to discount, clearly from kids. The rest we'll match against the parents. Whatever's left may be our man. However, Mrs Emerson says they have friends and family in and out of here all the time. 'Like a hotel' apparently. So it won't be easy."

It never was. Every job was an uphill battle as far as Blake was concerned.

"You'll pull it off though, Brian."

It was meant as mockery though Blake took it entirely at face value and responded with a stiffer spine and an appreciative grin.

"Where did Yvonne go?" asked Blake.

"Trying to find a mobile signal."

"Impossible here, the chalk blocks everything."

Blake missed the fact that Gray had been able to get through to him not so long ago. Hamson had promised Gray food if he managed Blake on her behalf.

"Well, give her my best, would you?"

"It would be my pleasure, Brian."

"Bloody gold dust these beach huts. Council charges a fortune for them yet the waiting lists are huge. I've been on it for years."

"I can't see what the fuss is all about. They're just sheds."

"It's Charles Dickens' fault, you know."

"What is, Brian?"

"Thanet's tourism, the boom and bust. You know he discovered Broadstairs walking here from Ramsgate? He would have passed the very beach those corpses washed up on."

Thankfully, Gray's mobile rang before Blake could give him more of a social history lesson, and again disproving Blake's assertion that mobile calls were impossible here. Gray answered, nodding a half-hearted apology at Blake.

"Morning, Sol." It was the boss, Carslake. "How's the beach?"

"Bracing."

Carslake's barking laugh was mercifully brief. "Just calling to get your thoughts on the bodies."

"Hasn't Yvonne filled you in?"

"I'd rather talk to a proper detective first."

Gray winced. Relations between Hamson and Carslake, never good to start with, had deteriorated further. She was running out of allies – given her interpersonal skills, she hadn't that many people on her side to start with. Gray gave Carslake a brief rundown of the situation and their latest findings.

"Such a pity about the boy," said Carslake when Gray had finished. Regan had to be well into his twenties. Hardly a boy. "What's next?"

"The death knock."

Carslake sighed. "Give Jake my condolences, would you?"

"Of course."

"Hang on; I've got another call coming in. Hamson again. Better take it this time." The line went dead before Gray could reply.

Gray put his phone away. He handed his business card to Mrs Emerson, said goodbye to Blake, then made the climb up the relatively short, though steep, incline to the road above. He was huffing by the time he reached the peak. Hamson was leaning against his vehicle, cigarette in one hand, mobile in the other. She nodded to indicate she'd seen him. By the time she finished talking the cigarette was done too.

"Just bringing Carslake up to date," she said. Gray didn't tell her he'd done exactly the same. Things were complicated enough already. "How did it go?"

"Might have found some fingerprints. I've called the station, told them to get legs out on the street, see if we can find our mystery man."

"Easier said than done," said Hamson. "Particularly if he gets to Margate." There was a large population of immigrants in the town and the description they had wasn't much to go on. "And Blake?"

"I did enough to earn my bacon."

"Makes a change," said Hamson. It seemed like she meant it.

Five

From the driver's seat, Gray wound down the passenger window and locked it open with the press of a button. Hamson glared at him. Gray preferred her indignation to the lingering stench of cigarette. The outcome of no longer being a smoker: love had turned into loathing.

In comparison, Hamson was smoking more than ever. Too much, Gray thought. She seemed to permanently have a lit cigarette between her fingers whenever they were away from the office. She was often to be found standing outside the station, puffing away. However, he kept his opinion to himself. It wasn't worth an ember in the eye.

In the ensuing flinty silence, they crossed the border from Broadstairs into Ramsgate. He followed Victoria Parade, houses one side, the coastline the other, until it became Wellington Crescent, a switchback hill which carried the road down to sea level. They passed a waterfall which was, as usual, more foam than flow because some local joker had again dumped a bottle of washing up liquid into the cascade.

Gray turned off at the bottom of the hill, driving past bars and restaurants which looked out onto yachts bobbing in the harbour. A hundred yards along, he pulled into a parking spot. There were a couple of bollards; otherwise it was a straightforward plunge into the still, black waters for the unwary or incompetent.

As Gray got out of the car he felt bile rise in his throat. He swallowed it down, coughed.

"Are you okay?" asked Hamson.

"Just indigestion," he croaked, a searing in his throat and chest.

"Again?"

"It's all this healthy living, Von."

"You should get it looked at."

"I'm fine." Gray led Hamson to their destination. Between a tall stone needle erected to commemorate Prince Albert, and the shut-down casino, stood a bright and shiny Dreamliner caravan, now converted into a burger van.

The proprietor, a curly haired young man, was leaning over a hot plate. He glanced up at Gray's arrival, stopped flipping meat patties. "What can I get you?"

"A burger, a bacon roll, and two coffees," said Gray.

"What about the diet?" asked Hamson.

Gray had been trying a health kick recently, although sticking to it had proven much harder than he'd thought it would be. "I can have a day off every now and again, can't I?"

"Some of us have willpower. Just the drink for me."

"You sure?"

"Very."

"Cancel the bacon roll then."

The proprietor nodded, told them to take a seat and handed over a small piece of paper with a number printed on it, even though there wasn't a queue.

"Can I get a cup of milk?" asked Gray.

"Of course." The man got a mug from beneath the counter and poured some from a plastic bottle. Gray swallowed the cold drink. It immediately soothed the pressure in his chest.

Hamson was sitting at one of the tables on the pavement. It was pleasant in the sunshine. Gray joined her, scattering a handful of pigeons and a seagull which were getting as near as they dared, on the hunt for any scraps of food.

"I can't believe you're eating here," said Hamson as she lit up. "It looks like a hygiene nightmare. And a burger, at this time of day."

"I've a cast-iron constitution."

Hamson snorted then blew smoke from her nostrils. "Tell me about Jake Armitage."

Gray shooed the birds away. "At one time or another Jake has owned pretty much every commercial property in the area. Mainly guest houses, bed and breakfasts, bedsits. Cheap digs that these days cater for the unemployed and underprivileged."

Hamson eyed Gray through curling smoke. "Low rent? Like for immigrants?"

"Precisely for immigrants."

"Coffee's ready," interrupted the proprietor. Gray collected the two steaming mugs and brought them back to the table.

"You wouldn't think there's much profit in it," said Hamson.

"The government pays, so there's plenty of money. He also owns a pub and the nightclub, Seagram's."

"I've had a few nights there. Seagram's is the opposite end of the scale, certainly not low rent given the prices at the bar."

"I wouldn't know, Von, I've never been in."

"They cater for the London set. And the pub?"

"The Mechanical Monkey." Upmarket and respectable – also did good food and wasn't far from where Jake lived. Gray and Jake drank in there many times when they were teenagers. Funny how the world turned.

"I've never heard of Jake until today," said Hamson.

"Unlikely you would have. But a decade ago he was infamous."

"Why?"

"He's always sailed close to the wind. Buildings he owned had a tendency to burn down at the most opportune moments."

"And he got away with it?"

"There was never any clear evidence of wrongdoing, just rumours. The last apparent accident was about the time Tom disappeared. Some people died."

"Were you involved in the investigation?"

"I wasn't really in the right frame of mind, but I read about it afterwards." Odd how after years of suppression recently he could discuss Tom without feeling so uptight. "The blaze took out a large guest house called Sunset. It transpired the building was blocking a development opportunity for an out of town company. Worse, Jake was apparently involved with them. He got an insurance payout and saved the expense of knocking the building down, allegedly. Seagram's is there now. I'd show you the original newspaper article. If I still had it." The article had been in a pile of documents Hamson confiscated from Gray.

"Sorry."

"Doesn't matter. History. Anyway, Jake had been a flamboyant character, happiest when on the front page of the local rag. The big fish in the small pond. He had a colourful private life too. Three marriages, three kids, three divorces. His last wife up and left him around the same time as the Sunset guest house fire, took the youngest child, a daughter. The two boys – Regan and Cameron – stayed. Her departure was different to the prior two. It was her choice, not his. The divorce and all the negative publicity around the fire hit Jake hard. He disappeared from view."

"He's a recluse?"

"Not as such, just departed the limelight."

The burger was ready as Gray's mobile rang. He recognised the number, sighed. He could ignore it, though he knew the caller would just keep trying until he picked up. Hamson collected the food while Gray answered.

"No comment," said Gray. He took a chunk out of the burger, chewed, and swallowed. The food stuck in his throat. He coughed, trying to clear the blockage.

The person on the other end gave a wheezing laugh. "There never is, Sergeant Gray," said William Noble, ex-editor-in-chief of the local newspaper, the *Thanet Echo*, now the overseer of a blog grandly called *Thanet's Voice*. He'd been around forever, knew everyone and, worst of all, was tenacious. "I'm calling about the bodies."

"What bodies, Will?"

Hamson frowned at Gray. He mouthed "Noble" and her scowl deepened.

"Come, come Solomon, spit it out. Someone will eventually, so why not you?"

"I've no idea what you're referring to."

"I hear of three corpses found on the beach. All drowned."

"If you say so." Gray was glad Noble didn't have all the details.

"No statement to make at all, Sergeant? I'll quote you as a source close to the police. We'll keep names out of it, of course." Noble laughed once more.

"Nice try, but no cigar this time."

"Ah well, had to give it a go. Almost impossible to get a scoop these days. See you at the protest march later?"

"What march?"

"Where have you been hiding the last few weeks? The attack on social care by the government and the impact it's having on service provision like the NHS can't be allowed to go on! We're demonstrating through Margate."

"I doubt I'll be able to make it."

"Knew you'd say that. It's only a little thing."

"Good luck." Gray disconnected, his mind on the fact that Noble would have the story on his blog soon, if not already.

"What did he want?" asked Hamson.

"Fishing. Interesting coincidence, though. Noble and Jake have history too. After the Sunset fire Jake sued over some articles Noble had run. Jake won, the *Thanet Echo* closed and Noble was out of a job."

"Small world we live in."

Gray nodded. "Suppose we'd better go." He swallowed a mouthful of coffee and grabbed the burger. He had a huge bite of the bread as he unlocked the car. Hamson cringed at the sight. "What? A man's got to eat."

Six

"He lives here?" asked Hamson as Gray turned through a gap between high flint walls. What had been terraced houses along a narrow thoroughfare looming over the car, became a spacious static mobile home estate.

"He has to live somewhere."

"In a caravan?"

"Your observational skills do you proud, Von. Though strictly it's a mobile home."

"It's a caravan."

Gray belched. "Sorry." His stomach grumbled. He'd begun to feel ill on the drive over. "Not sure about that burger."

"I told you."

Gray parked beside a Rolls Royce with a private licence plate – Jake's. Gray wouldn't be bothering to lock his car. In comparison to the Rolls it was too old and crap. Before they got out, Gray put a restraining hand on Hamson's forearm. "Don't rise to anything he says."

She frowned. "Why?"

"He'll attempt to pull your strings. King-sized arsehole, remember?"

"Worried he'll set me on fire?"

"More the other way around."

Hamson snorted.

Despite appearances, this was prime real estate. It possessed a fantastic view over the U-shaped Pegwell Bay into which the Great Stour River emptied. When the tide turned it did so with vengeance, the North Sea receding for at least a mile and exposing a huge expanse of mud, giving a window of a couple of hours for a handful of industrious men to dig for lugworms, the last few of a dying trade.

On the far side of the bay were the chimneys and buildings of the old Pfizer industrial site, mainly mothballed now. Atop the tip of the sweep, Deal Pier stretched out, beyond which was the port of Dover, hidden from view. The static homes provided a decent income too, Gray would bet. And Jake owned the whole site.

It took Gray a moment to remember which home was Jake's before he led Hamson to a green rectangular box. Wooden blinds obscured the systematically spaced windows. A reasonable-sized garden of grass and flower borders extended all around it, enclosed by a waist-high, white-painted wooden picket fence.

Hamson leaned over and made a show of peering intently into the garden. "Pity," she said.

"What is?" Gray knew he shouldn't ask.

"No gnomes."

"Such a stereotypical attitude from an officer of the law."

"What do you expect?"

Gray walked up a couple of steps and rapped on the caravan's frosted glass door. Within seconds it opened – outwards. He moved back to avoid being struck. Above Gray stood a casually dressed young man, brown hair tousled, unshaven. Not quite as good-looking as his recently deceased brother. This was the other son, Cameron.

"Is your dad in? I need a word."

"Who are you?"

"An old friend."

Cameron laughed. "Jake doesn't have any friends."

Jake? "Your dad will want to see us."

"Is everything okay? You don't look well."

"Your father, please."

Cameron shrugged. "Sure." He stepped outside and closed the door behind him. "Excuse me." Gray and Hamson parted and Cameron slid through.

He led them to what was the original building, once a farm by the look of it. A single-storey lean-to, set mostly to glass, was propped against the red stone wall. It possessed an uninterrupted view of the bay through sensibly aligned mobile homes.

Cameron pointed. "The Club House. You'll find Jake inside."

"Where are your toilets?" asked Gray. He was going to throw up any moment.

"There." Cameron nodded to a door beside the Club House. Gray ran. He barely managed to get inside a stall before he voided the contents of his stomach. He flushed a couple of times, then went to the sinks and laid his forehead against the wall-mounted mirror until his head stopped spinning.

He turned on the cold tap, washed his hands and face, dried them. Unsteadily, he left the toilets. Hamson was outside the door.

"You look awful," said Cameron who'd stuck around to keep Hamson company.

"I'm feeling better now."

"Told you that place was a hygiene nightmare," said Hamson. "Are you ready for this?"

"As I'll ever be."

Cameron opened the door for them. Basically, the Club House was a bar, with Jake its only patron. He was sitting in t-shirt and shorts at a table, feet up on a chair opposite, reading a newspaper. It was warm because of all the glass. The cane furniture with floral cushions would suit a conservatory. An empty cup sat on a pine table in front of Jake. He ignored them and focused on the article.

"Jake," said Cameron. "Some people are here to see you."

"Will I ever get you to call me Dad?" asked Jake, keeping his eyes down.

Cameron smiled and shook his head.

"Hello, Jake," said Gray.

Now Jake lifted his head. His face split into a wide grin. He stood, dropped the newspaper into his vacated seat and crossed to Gray. "Solomon Gray, as I live and breathe." He took Gray's hand and squeezed. Just a little too hard. "You look like shit."

"Thanks."

Jake was a short man, no more than five-and-a-half feet. Both Gray and Hamson stood head and shoulders above him. He was broad with it too, given to muscle rather than fat. Jake clearly kept himself fit. His stomach was flat, and his arms bulged.

"How many years has it been?"

"I don't want to think about it."

Jake let go of Gray. "And DI Hamson as well," he said, shaking her hand now. "I knew today would be a good one as soon as I woke up."

"I don't believe we've met before, Mr Armitage."

"I make it my business to know all the movers and shakers in Thanet, even if it is from afar. Sit down and take a load off. What would you like to drink?"

"Orange juice," said Hamson.

Jake manoeuvred himself behind the bar which was another strip of pine, heavily lacquered, parallel to the windows. There were a couple of handles to pump beer and a limited row of optics on the wall – gin, whisky, brandy. Gray took his coat off; it was like a greenhouse in here.

"Can you make mine water?" asked Gray.

"Not drinking, Sol?"

"I've been cutting back."

Jake slapped his forehead. "Of course, stupid of me. After your troubles a few months ago. It was all over the papers."

"I'm on duty."

Jake nodded. "Fair enough." He turned to his son. "Cameron?"

"I'll leave you to it," he said.

"Nonsense, stay. Anything our good friends here have to say I'm sure you can hear." Jake's tone left no room for argument.

"Sparkling water, then."

"I'll join you, I think." Jake leaned beneath the bar and came back with a bottle of orange and two large bottles of water. They went onto a tray, along with four glasses and a bucket of ice.

"I told you, sit down!" said Jake with a grin as he carried the tray over. "You there, Sol. And this one is for you, inspector." Jake directed them to a comfortable seat and a stool respectively, giving Gray a place to his right looking outwards towards the sky and Hamson to the left, facing the bar. Cameron took an armchair.

"So this isn't a social visit, then?" said Jake.

"No," said Gray.

"What, then? Somebody died?" Jake grinned.

There was a pause.

"Yes," said Hamson eventually.

"Regan. We found him earlier this morning," said Gray.

"This is a joke, right?"

"No, Mr Armitage. Sadly, it isn't," said Hamson.

"Is it true, Sol?"

"It's true," said Hamson.

Jake twisted, stuck a finger out at Gray. "I asked him, not you."

Gray said, "I'm sorry to say it is."

"You have our condolences," said Hamson.

"Keep your fucking sympathy," snarled Jake.

"It's not DI Hamson's fault," said Cameron who had tears in his eyes.

Jake glared at Cameron momentarily, nodded and turned to Hamson. "I'm sorry, that was uncalled for."

Cameron stood up, went to the bar, grabbed a whisky bottle and a tumbler. He brought both back to the table, poured Jake a large dram and passed it to him. "Drink this, Dad." Cameron poured one for himself too. "I can't believe he's gone." Cameron sat back down, still holding the whisky bottle.

Jake took the glass and sank the measure in one, grimacing with the taste. Gray knew Jake well enough that he wouldn't want to show emotion in front of a cop. "What happened?" asked Jake.

"We're not sure yet, the investigation has only just got under way," said Hamson.

"Don't screw around. Just give it to me."

Hamson told Jake the basics. Jake didn't speak for a while afterwards, his forehead creased with a frown. "I don't get it," he eventually said. "Regan hated the sea. Even as a kid he was scared of it."

"It appears he was running migrants," said Gray.

"Migrants?" Jake shook his head. "That makes no sense."

"What did Regan do for money?"

"He worked for me, sort of. He's listed as a director of the business though it's a largely pointless role. He never actually came to work; it just meant I could pay him something. He wasn't good at holding down a job. Never saw the sense in hard work for commensurate reward. He expected success to come to him, rather than the other way around."

"When did you last see him?"

"Yesterday afternoon. Regan lives here, on site. I saw him park his car, then head to his place. Then he left again, later on."

"What time?"

"About six. He was done up for one of his usual Saturday nights out. Regan always hit the town on the weekend." Jake paused for a moment. "Listen to me; I'm already talking about him in the past tense."

"I know this is difficult, Jake, but do you know where he would have gone?"

"Not really, but he typically ended up at the club."

"Seagram's?"

"Yes."

"Was he there yesterday?"

"I didn't see him, but that doesn't mean anything. I'm always busy, particularly at the weekend."

"Do you have CCTV?"

"Of course."

"Do you mind if we send someone by to pick up the recordings?"

"No problem."

"We'll need to take a look around his caravan."

"Do whatever you need to."

"What about you, Cameron? When was your last sighting of your brother?"

"Half-brother. Same father, different mother. Same as Dad – here, yesterday."

"Why doesn't Cameron show you Regan's home now, DI Hamson?" asked Jake, butting in.

Hamson appeared only too pleased to leave. Cameron left the whisky behind.

When the door was closed, Jake said, "You need to keep her in line, Sol."

"She's my boss. We operate to a different set of rules than you. We always have."

"I remember, that was part of the problem."

Gray held his tongue. The pair had been friends at school, Jake the firebrand, Gray the hanger-on. As they'd grown up, Gray developed a law-abiding persona, whereas Jake stayed true to his roots. When Gray joined the police the two drifted further apart.

"I don't understand any of this, Sol. It makes no sense at all. Find out, will you? I'll make it worth your while."

"It's my job, Jake. I don't want your money."

"Of course, I keep forgetting."

"No, you don't."

"Touché."

"One other thing. Someone will need to identify the body."

"Christ." Jake ran a hand over his face. "This isn't what I expected my day to consist of."

"Sorry, Jake."

"Not your fault."

"When can you come down?"

"Just give me half an hour, okay? I'll require some further fortification." Jake raised the whisky glass.

"Get Cameron to drive you. It wouldn't be good to be arrested for drunk driving."

"In the scheme of things I couldn't give a shit, Sol."

"I'd better get going."

At the door, Jake stopped Gray. "Thanks for being here. I won't forget." There were tears in his eyes.

"You never do."

"I'll take that as a compliment."

"Here. In case you need anything." Gray passed over his card.

Gray closed the door softly behind him. He wound his way between the rows of caravans until he found Cameron propped up against one, arms crossed.

"She's inside," said Cameron. He looked to the Club House at the sound of breaking glass. "I think I'll leave Jake to it for now."

"I've a couple more questions for you, Cameron."

"Shoot."

"Do you work for your father as well?"

"Yes, although I earn my keep, at least."

"And you live here too?"

"No, I don't have one of these wonderful abodes. I manage the site for Jake. If I was here all the time it would drive me mad, and it wasn't me Jake needed to keep an eye on. I have one of the flats on Marine Esplanade in Ramsgate. I surf and jet-ski so it's the perfect location. When I'm not working I'm out on the water."

Hamson stepped out of the mobile home. "I've had a quick look around," she said, taking off her blue nitrile gloves. She stuffed them in her pocket. "Can't see anything obvious."

"Forensics can do some deeper digging." Gray turned to Cameron. "Thanks for your time, Cameron, and again, our condolences." Gray shook Cameron's hand. He and Hamson headed back to the car.

"We might as well go straight to the mortuary," said Gray. "Jake said he'd be over shortly. Otherwise, by the time we reach the station we'll be leaving again."

"Good idea."

Gray started the engine and reversed out of the spot. Cameron was still leaning against his brother's caravan, watching them as they drove out through the high walls.

"Did you learn anything else from Jake?" asked Hamson.

"Not much." Gray told her what he had said.

"You two, though," said Hamson after a moment's pause.
"What?"
"You were like old bloody mates."
That was about right.
Bloody mates.

Seven

Adnan Khoury walked quickly, head down, avoiding the few people he saw, sticking to the shoreline. His progress brought him into a built-up area. A road sign said Margate. Buildings meant people, which was good and bad. In the distance he could hear shouts, whistles, and chants. He passed a lifeboat station, the doors open, a boat on a trolley. A man in yellow oilskins wiping his hands onto a cloth didn't give Khoury a second glance.

He carried on for a few hundred yards before pausing at the edge of a harbour, an inner bay protected by a long concrete arm. Here the town opened up. Margate had a shabby appearance. Before him, was a road lined with pubs, cafés, restaurants and, beyond, an amusement park called Dreamland, which seemed to be mainly bright, flashing lights even though it was mid-morning. Then a tall block of flats which loomed like a dirty iceberg.

Now he could see what the noise was about. A protest march making its way along the road. Lots of people, banners held high, words Khoury couldn't read. Somebody at the front on a megaphone, chanting. The line stretched on back down the sea front. Dotted periodically were fluorescent yellow jackets and uniforms; apparently the police.

Khoury headed along the harbour arm, away from the march. At the far end was a bench. He sat down. While

Khoury waited, he thought about his brother Najjar and friend Shadid. What had happened to them after Khoury threw himself off the boat and swum for shore? Najjar had been stabbed, that much he knew.

He could have lost it there and then. The grief he'd been bottling up for the last few hours threatened to spill over. A moan escaped his lips. Khoury glanced over his shoulder to see if anyone had heard. He was alone. Khoury allowed himself a few moments to think about Najjar. He rocked back and forth, arms across his chest, head bowed. Tears ran down his cheeks.

The irony of it all. Najjar had been the kind-hearted brother, always with a good word for people, a helping hand. Khoury was the black sheep. He'd needed to leave Syria. Najjar only came along to protect him, Shadid too, as a family favour. Khoury was desperate to speak with his wife – to see how his little girl was handling her chemo treatments. It had been a week since they'd last spoken. He supposed they were still in hospital. At least they were safe while he was away. And soon, they could join him in England, or that had been the plan.

For now, all he wanted to do was scream. But it wouldn't do well to draw attention to himself. There would be people after him.

Khoury had to acquire the basics – clothes, food, money – and soon. He needed somewhere to sleep, too. If it was to be the streets, he needed the means.

It took about twenty minutes for the demonstrators to pass. His stomach rumbled. He was starving. Only some stale biscuits in the last twenty-four hours. Luckily Khoury was wiry, not an ounce of fat on him; he didn't need to eat a great deal to survive.

Once the protesters were just a trickle and the police had gone, Khoury made his way to the road which ran parallel with the sea front. A long line of cars followed in the march's wake. Pedestrians on the pavements went about their business. None gave him even a first glance.

Margate reminded Khoury of Calais, where there was also a brooding sense of acceptance between locals and immigrants. He'd blend in here, for sure.

He wandered the pedestrianised shopping area, getting a feel for the immediate surroundings. He stole an apple from a fruit and vegetable shop, picking it up from a tray as he passed. When he was down to the core, his hunger awoken rather than satisfied, he selected his first target, a cheap clothing store. He entered through large, heavy doors and mooched the racks of low cost garments. He was pleased to see there weren't any electronic tags.

First, he picked up a jacket, something long and heavy with a hood. When he was sure no one was looking he slipped it on, alert and ready to run. No alarms were raised. Emboldened, he carried on with his spree, picking up some pants and socks. Upstairs was a food section. He put a few easily concealed items in his pockets; high-energy chocolate bars and drinks. Finally, just before leaving, he lifted a hoodie from a coat hanger and concealed it beneath the coat.

Holding the hoodie under his jacket he was almost on the street when a hand fell on his shoulder.

"Where do you think you're going?"

Khoury turned. A man, frowning at him, dressed normally, not a guard in a uniform. Khoury couldn't reach his knife; it was tucked away below what were now several layers of clothes.

He tried to shrug the hand off, but the man gripped the coat tighter, spun Khoury ninety degrees and pulled him around the corner, away from the store.

"You were lucky you didn't get caught," said the man. Khoury had the chance to properly look at him. He was young, blonde hair twisted into dreadlocks. He wore a camouflage army jacket covered in badges and Doc Marten boots.

"You're new here, right?"

Khoury's understanding of English was good. In his past life back home he'd been a language teacher in adult education.

Khoury nodded. What was going on?

The young man sighed. "Look, you need to keep your head down." He dipped into Khoury's pockets, pulled out the chocolate bars, put them back in again. "Getting done for this isn't worth it. You'll be on a boat and back to France for less. I haven't got much myself, but here you go." He held up a five-pound note. "Have you got anywhere to sleep?"

Khoury shook his head but didn't take the cash, dubious as to how the young man would expect him to earn it. But the young man stuffed the note into one of Khoury's pockets.

He said, "There's a place called the Lighthouse Project. They've got beds and food. Would you like me to show you where it is?"

"Yes."

"Follow me."

The young man led Khoury out of the alley, turned, and walked up the slope towards the centre of town. They'd only gone about a hundred yards when Khoury stopped dead. The television in the shop window had caught his eye.

Not wanting to believe what he was seeing, Khoury went up to the window, bumping into a passer-by in the process, sending her bags spilling to the ground. Khoury barely noticed.

He pressed his palms up against the glass as the camera view panned over a building in ruins. Massive slabs of shattered concrete and twisted metal. Clearly it had once been a large construction, now reduced to rubble.

"What's the matter?" asked the young man, standing by Khoury's side. Khoury ignored him.

A legend appeared on the screen, revealing the location as a children's hospital in the rebel-held Idlib province. The Syrian regime, supported by the Russians, had been indiscriminately attacking rebel-held facilities.

Khoury sagged to his knees. There was only one children's hospital in Idlib. It was where his daughter was being treated. Laila. She would be dead. His wife, too. There was no way she would have left his daughter's side. They were dead, both of them. Khoury was alone. Tears flowed down his face. He felt a hand fall on his shoulder.

"Bastards," said the young man.

Something hardened inside Khoury then. His people had suffered so much. He stood, cuffed away the tears. "Please take me to the refuge," he said. The young man stared at Khoury for a long moment before he nodded.

Eight

Standing in the mortuary viewing room, Solomon Gray understood how Jake was feeling. Hollowed-out cheeks, pallid skin, and haunted eyes were just the outward, visible display of the gut-wrenching sense of loss. Gray knew because he'd felt exactly the same when he stood above the body of his ex-wife after she'd committed suicide.

However, there was one critical difference. Jake was about to view his dead child. There could be nothing worse for a parent. At least Gray hadn't had to suffer that.

Yet.

Gray believed that Tom was still out there somewhere, waiting to be found. He hadn't received the solid, irrevocable proof that Tom was deceased, the way Jake was about to. Tom would be on the edge of tipping into adulthood now. Seventeen. Maybe unaware of his background, except perhaps for a few, nagging memories that clung to his subconscious like a fading dream.

Cameron was here, as a crutch for his father; and the pathologist Ben Clough, to gain official confirmation of the identity of the corpse.

And, of course, Regan, stretched out on a gurney, a distinct form beneath a white sheet.

"Are you ready?" asked Clough. He stood by Regan's head, Jake further down at chest height, Cameron parallel to his father on the other side of his half-brother, Gray at the bottom of the gurney where he could see both of the Armitages' expressions.

Jake visibly drew in a breath, his chest swelling. He exhaled, nodded. Delicately, Clough pinched both sides of the sheet between finger and thumb and peeled the shroud off the corpse. Clough exposed face and shoulders. Naked, pallid skin, bloodless lips, eyes closed.

Regan was calm in death. Though Gray imagined his last moments were anything but. Being thrust underwater by successive waves, thrashing, hunting for air. The searing pain across his lungs and heart as they starved of oxygen. Perhaps at the end, the relief was blessed.

More often than not, bereaved relatives viewing a loved one collapsed as grief overtook them. Not Jake. His stance stiffened; he stood taller, stronger when he laid eyes on his son, whereas Cameron remained expressionless.

Jake turned to Clough. "It's him."

"I'm sorry for your loss," said Clough.

Jake took a step forward. He raised a hand as if to stroke his son's face, then drew it back and, before Gray could stop him, slapped Regan on the cheek, following up with another strike. Cameron and Gray leapt forward at the same time. Cameron reached Jake first, and got an arm around a shoulder. Jake shook him off and managed to strike Regan again. Gray and Cameron took a grip of Jake, barging him backwards like they were in a rugby match until he was against a wall. He was strong though, and fought against them.

"Dad!" shouted Cameron. "Stop it!"

"He's an idiot!" shouted Jake.

"Calm down, Jake," said Gray.

Clough, after initially freezing in surprise at the turn of events, covered up Regan with the sheet once more and slid the gurney back into the wall. As soon as he did so, Gray felt Jake's muscles relax.

"Are we done?" asked Gray.

Jake nodded. "Sorry, I don't know what came over me. You can let go."

"Get him out of here," said Gray to Cameron, who nodded.

When the Armitages had left, Clough said, "Well, that was a first."

"Good thinking, getting rid of the body."

"I didn't know what else to do."

Gray let go of a lungful of air, felt himself relax too. "When's the PM?"

"Tomorrow, first thing."

Gray said his goodbyes, left the suite, found Hamson hovering by a vending machine. She folded up the packet of crisps she'd been eating and shoved it into a pocket. Cheese and onion, he reckoned by the smell. At least she didn't lick her fingers.

"How did it go?" asked Hamson.

Gray fell in step beside her and told her what happened.

"Really? I've never heard of that reaction before."

"That's what Clough said."

"I may put you down for the PM."

"Great."

"No need to thank me."

"I wasn't planning to."

Hamson's phone rang at the car which was parked right in front of the entrance. She handed Gray the keys while she spoke. He unlocked and got inside, waiting for her. He didn't have to wait long.

"That was Mike," she said, joining him in the car. "Says he's got some CCTV we need to see."

Gray drove slowly through the car park. When they were on the main road Hamson said, "What about Cameron?"

"He was controlled. He said and did nothing until Jake lost it."

"The reaction of a grieving relative?"

"Maybe."

Nine

Then
Regan Armitage stepped back into the shadow of a shop entrance, warned by the shout.

"Rachel!"

A girl ran past on the other side of the road. A man and a woman stood on the top step of the Sunset guest house. The man shouted again. But Rachel, whoever she was, got lost in the gloom.

Regan stayed still; wondered if he should come back tomorrow. The point of arriving at this time of night was that everybody should be asleep. After a few minutes of indecision, he watched the pair go back inside. Another minute and the light in the downstairs bay window switched off. Regan breathed a sigh of relief. He leaned out from the darkness, looked up and down the road, saw no one. He decided to wait another quarter of an hour.

The minutes ticked slowly past, Regan expecting someone to happen by and ask him what he was doing. But no one did. When the time was up, Regan hefted the heavy backpack from the ground, the strap cutting into his shoulder. Quickly he walked the hundred yards or so to the guest house and turned into the dark, narrow alley which ran alongside it.

A wooden fence separated garden from alley. A few days ago, he'd loosened a couple of the boards. He bent over, got his fingers around the edge of the rotting wood. He was relieved when both came away easily. He shoved the backpack through and then, after a glance up and down the alley, followed it.

Regan found himself in a long, narrow back yard. Like the girl, he paused, listened. Nothing. No noise, no light spilling out of any windows. He smelt engine oil. Under a tarpaulin was an old motorbike. He carried the pack to the back door. He knelt down and nudged at a cat flap in the door. It moved freely. He quietly unzipped the pack and pulled out a plastic jerry can, the kind drivers use as emergency back-up. He unscrewed the cap; took a wooden lolly stick from an inside pocket, and wedged the flap open with it.

The cat chose then to exit, pushing its way out through the hole. It was a tight squeeze. The animal rubbed itself against Regan. He stroked it briefly before tipping the contents of the jerry can through the flap into the room beyond.

The petrol fumes were powerful. Got right up Regan's nose. Felt like the gas was scraping his sinuses, making him feel giddy and nauseous at the same time. The cat didn't like it either and backed away. Regan poured until the can was empty. Next, he pulled some rags out of the bag and laid them on the tiled floor.

Regan took his final tool. A brass Zippo lighter. It was a beautiful object; Regan flicked the wheel and the gas caught, producing a yellow flame. He lit a rag and, when it was burning, dropped the lighter inside. Immediately the flames expanded, a wave of blue rushing across the kitchen floor. For a moment, Regan watched – transfixed by the beauty – until, behind him, the cat hissed. Regan turned and saw the animal dive through the gap in the fence, back lit by the blaze. Alert now, Regan grabbed the backpack and hustled too.

In the alley, Regan glanced over his shoulder. He was shocked by how quickly the fire had taken. He could see the flames. He'd need to be quick. Walking as fast as he dared without bringing attention to himself he soon arrived at the phone box. The hinges squeaked as the door opened and closed. He lifted the receiver. His plan was to ring the fire brigade so the conflagration would be put out, but not so soon that the house itself could be saved. It would mean the guest house was out of business – which was the objective.

When Regan put the receiver to his ear, however, he heard nothing. He rattled at the contacts. Still silence. He looked down. The cord had been cut. The panic bloomed in his gut. There was no way he'd be making the call from here.

He left the phone box and began running...

Ten

N**ow** The traffic in front of Gray slowed before it ground to a halt. He was most of the way along Belgrave Road, a tributary which connected with the Margate seafront and ran along the border of the Dreamland amusement park.

"What's going on?" asked Hamson. They were less than a mile from the station now, just a few minutes' stop-start drive under normal conditions.

"I've no idea," said Gray. The car in front rolled forward a few feet then paused again. The road could be busy, but a dead halt was unusual.

"We need to be at the station as soon as."

"I know." Gray lowered his window. He could hear whistles and shouting. He popped open his door and got out. Several other motorists were standing beside their cars too. There was a thick line of people walking past the bottom of Belgrave Road, many holding flags and banners. A few drivers performed a one-hundred-and-eighty-degree turn and swung back the way they'd come.

Gray bent down and stuck his head inside the car. "It must be the protest march Noble mentioned."

"What protest march?"

"Apparently it's to do with the squeeze on social services or something."

"And you knew about this?"

"Vaguely."

"Christ, we could have come in via Cliftonville and avoided all this. Do you know what route they're taking?"

"I've no idea."

"We can't sit around here all day. Dump the car somewhere and we'll walk."

A space had opened up in front of Gray. He manoeuvred until he could bump the car up the kerb and out the way. He locked up once Hamson was on the pavement and they got walking. A little further on, there was a knot of people gathered outside a house. As they neared, a portly man sporting a shock of white hair and goatee with pince nez glasses perched on his nose stepped forward and blocked their way.

It was William Noble. "You made it then!" he said.

"Just passing through," said Gray.

"You need to stay; this is an important issue which will affect everyone eventually. Services are getting squeezed all over the place." Noble pointed at the house, a large and intricate gold ring glinted on his index finger. A sign above the doorway named it as the Lighthouse Project, a drop-in centre for the homeless. "It's just the start, I'm telling you. We have to draw the line, right here, right now. They're trying to close this place down, build houses or shops on it."

"Who is?"

"The corporate machine." When he saw his answer was too obtuse for Gray, Noble clarified, "A London mob called Millstone Property Developers."

"Never heard of them."

"Oh, they're everywhere. Like most companies, it's profit first, people third." Noble turned away, returning with a placard. "I've got a spare."

"I can't," said Gray. "I need to get going." Hamson had barely paused for the interruption and was fast receding. "Got to go, Will."

Noble put an arm out and stopped Gray. "I heard one of the dead was Regan Armitage."

"I can't comment."

"Call me when you can." Noble let go.

Gray caught up with Hamson at the intersection of Belgrave Road and the esplanade. He was amazed to see so many people. It was noisy too; repetitive chanting and ear-piercing whistles. The line wound up the hill and away from them. While Gray stood observing, someone pushed a leaflet into his hand. It was a flier about the impact of the proposed closures.

After a pause, Hamson impatiently forced her way through the crowd. Gray shoved the paper into his pocket and followed, ignoring the complaints of those she barged out of her way.

"Bloody do-gooders," said Hamson once they were on the other side and free.

"That's democracy for you," said Gray.

MIKE FOWLER WAS SEATED at his desk in the detectives' office when Gray and Hamson arrived, Carslake at Fowler's shoulder. The CCTV footage was frozen on a wall-mounted TV screen and ready to go.

"Where have you been?" asked Fowler.

Hamson held up a hand. "Don't."

She positioned herself to leave a gap for Gray between herself and Carslake.

"Get started, Mike," said Carslake.

"I picked up the footage from the Broadstairs Town Hall," said Fowler. "There isn't any CCTV on the beach, just along the clifftop, in the town, and on the jetty itself."

Fowler clicked the mouse button and the scene began to play. The perspective was across Viking Bay, back towards Dumpton Gap. Cliffs in the distance, sea to one side, sand to the other. A canoeist was battling the surf, and on dry land somebody was throwing a stick for a dog. The picture quality was poor: grainy black and white.

"Where are we looking?" asked Carslake.

Fowler stood up and tapped the screen. "Here, the central figure."

In the expanse, moving with unpractised difficulty along the shoreline, was a figure. The person stayed right against the water's edge, head down, growing in size as the distance shortened. At the foot of the jetty the man paused and glanced around, clearly deciding which route to take.

The esplanade led around between a pub called the Tartar Frigate and the old harbour building, a double-storey wooden construct, tilted over from hundreds of years of being battered by the wind. The other way was a steep hill to an old portcullis and back into town.

The man began walking again, drifting out of sight momentarily as he passed under the camera. The shot cut as they switched between perspectives. Now he was moving away from them. The man turned left and disappeared out of sight behind a toilet block – tall terraced houses in the background.

"Where did he go?" asked Hamson.

"Watch," he said. After a minute or so the man reappeared. "He went to the public toilets." The man was obscured from the lens once more. Another shot revealed him walking quickly through the car park behind the harbour building and receding along the esplanade. Fowler paused the footage. "No more cameras."

"In all likelihood, he headed our way then," said Gray.

"Certainly looks like that," said Hamson.

"Pity we don't have a better picture of him."

"Maybe we do," said Fowler. He sat down, hit a few buttons, and a close-up of the suspect popped up on screen. "I pulled this from the Tartar Frigate. They've got good quality lenses."

There was an image of their target, a side-on view of a man with dark skin, a beard, and a prominent nose. It wasn't great, though it was enough to go on. Fowler passed over a handful of printouts.

"Good job, Mike," said Carslake and patted him on the shoulder. "Can you send copies of everything to my office please, Yvonne? Top brass are all over this, and I need to brief them accordingly."

"Of course, sir," said Hamson.

Carslake left the room.

At his desk, Gray took the flier out of his pocket and glanced over it. A handful of inflammatory statements studded with exclamation marks, some photos of rough sleepers, and people in hospital. On the back the company Noble had mentioned, Millstone, got another mention and not a positive one. They were being blamed for profiting by others' misfortunes.

"Sol," said Hamson. "Incident Room, now. We've got work to do."

Gray threw the leaflet in the bottom drawer of his desk and followed Hamson.

Eleven

The incident room was buzzing, the activity centred around the murder board in the rectangular, high-ceilinged space. The board summarised all the pertinent information for clarity.

The same facts and suppositions would also be stored on the HOLMES2 database, an acronym for the second iteration of the "Home Office Large Major Enquiry System". But during a major investigation the online data quickly became large and unwieldy, difficult to see the detail in the morass of information being added by multiple people. Too many strands to focus on. The board was the concise fulcrum around which the investigation would rotate. Everything relevant to the case in one place, a visual aid.

Otherwise, the incident room was sounds and movement. Ringing phones, cops talking to one another, talking to potential witnesses. Sifting, analysing, testing. Gray threaded through the desks, heading for the board.

Gray stood beside Hamson. He recognised Fowler's surprisingly neat script, all curves and loops, which crabbed down delineated columns. There were sections for each victim, possible motives, possible offenders, murder weapon. So far, the victims were marked only by their photographs and the legend "Unidentified". Three faces, all in death. At least one murdered.

Regan Armitage's section was brimming with facts and several suppositions. In comparison, the segment reserved for the beach hut intruder was empty except for Fowler's CCTV photo which he stuck up.

"We need to find this guy," said Hamson, tapping the mystery man. "He could be the key."

"Heads up, Von," said Fowler.

Gray turned. The station's Press Officer, Bethany Underwood, had entered the room. She was tall, skinny, and had frizzy bleached-blonde hair, thinning because she'd applied the chemicals too often. Underwood always seemed to be running on the edge, tense and stressed. She glanced around, spotted Hamson, and made her way straight over.

"We've got a problem," she said when six feet away. Underwood always got straight to the point.

"Oh?" said Hamson.

"Your case, I'm getting calls from the papers and TV, more and more of them. All wanting an update. Carslake's in my ear too. What shall I tell them?" Underwood glanced at the photos of the dead men. She began to chew at a nail, saw Fowler watching and quickly dropped her hand.

"I'm just about to carry out a briefing. Why don't you stay and listen, then we can talk after?"

"Okay, thanks." Underwood moved away, distancing herself from the victims. She stood by the large television screen.

"Everyone," said Hamson. She remained before the murder board and raised her voice. "Can I have your attention, please?"

Hamson allowed the noise to fall to a level where she could speak, rather than shout. A DC remained on the phone, quietly finishing a call.

"As you all know, this morning we found the body of Regan Armitage on a beach. He appears to have drowned. We also discovered two other men, one stabbed. The other appears to also have drowned, seemingly after a failed attempt to cross from France in a people-smuggling exercise. It is highly probable that another man survived the trip. This man was found sleeping in a nearby beach hut."

Hamson tapped the photo on the board, and it flicked up onto the TV screen so everybody could see. Heads turned towards it. Hamson continued, "It is critical we find him. he may be our key. Get his description out to uniform; I want everybody looking for him. And send pictures of the unknowns over to Interpol and French police. Let's see if we can get a match on them."

"Already done," said Fowler.

"Good, thanks, Mike. Now, Regan Armitage." Hamson pointed to his section on the board. "What was he doing in the last few hours of his life? Where had he been? Was he with anybody? We believe he was at Seagram's later in the evening. Again, we need to check CCTV. Cause of death has to be established for certain. Sol, you get the post mortem.

"Now, I don't need to tell any of you that this is a high-profile case. The son of a well-known local businessman, dead under mysterious circumstances. The media is already onto it, so are the powers that be. So, bring me everything and anything you find. Okay?" Hamson got nods from around the room. "Right, everyone, back to work."

Hamson made her way over to Underwood who, if anything, appeared more anxious. En-route, Hamson was stopped by a DC in his second year at CID, still keen and young.

They engaged in an animated discussion frustrating Underwood even more. Hamson stretched out a hand, touched the DC on the arm before she carried on. The DC went bright red, glanced around the office and turned a further, deeper shade of embarrassment when he clocked Gray and Fowler watching him.

"Someone needs to have a chat," said Fowler. "Warn him off."

Gray knew what that meant. The DC would be subjected to Fowler's cigarette-ash breath in his face as he loomed over the love-struck younger man and gave him the benefit of his wizened knowledge. It wasn't something Gray wanted to experience.

"I'll talk to him," said Gray.

"Why?"

"He's more likely to listen to me."

Fowler snorted, but seemed to accept the offer. "By the way, I was thinking. We should go out for a drink, just you and me. Like the old days."

Fowler's offer caught Gray by surprise.

Gray wondered if this was Hamson's doing. Fowler was peering at him expectantly. "Sure, just let me know when." Gray wondered if they'd ever actually get around to it. Words and deeds ...

"There's a pub quiz coming up, how about that?"

"Sounds good."

"Sol." It was Hamson, beckoning him over. She was with Underwood. Gray joined them. Hamson looked Gray up and down. "Have you got a tie?"

Gray groaned. That meant only one thing, a journalist briefing.

"Why me?" asked Gray.

"Because you're photogenic," said Hamson.

"Bullshit."

"Guilty as charged."

Gray rubbed his stomach, making exaggerated circular movements. "I feel ill again."

"Really." Hamson sounded totally unconvinced. "This is important, Sol, and you're my number two. We need to find the missing man. Bethany says the media is keen, so let's use them, okay?"

"Okay," said Gray, grudgingly.

"Thirty minutes enough?"

Gray nodded. "I'll find my best bib and tucker."

Before doing so, Gray headed off to find Carslake. He wanted to know more about the Dover witness who'd passed along the information on Tom, and Carslake hadn't yet given him the details. He took the stairs two at a time. In recent weeks he'd altered a number of elements about his life, cutting back on the rubbish that went into his body and burning off calories through exercise. The latter wasn't so difficult; he'd always preferred to walk instead of drive anyway. Reducing the alcohol and nicotine had been the tougher challenges to face up to. It had worked, though. The weight had been falling off.

"Afternoon, Sylvia," said Gray to Carslake's hoary administrator who he always made a point of being irritatingly sugar-sweet to. Sylvia barely acknowledged Gray, who was not her favourite person by any stretch of the imagination. Her false fingernails rattled at the keyboard. Each week she had her talons done. Typically in an unusual colour and decorated with some bling. This week was green with a silver arc across them. "Nice nails."

"The DCI's not in," said Sylvia. She picked up some headphones from her desk, put the buds into her ears, and pressed the screen on her phone. Gray heard tinny music. He sarcastically waved at her and left.

Gray had some smartening up to do.

Twelve

DCI Jeff Carslake watched the other car pull up to his bumper in the rearview mirror. It parked so close that when Jake stepped out and walked over, Carslake could only see the lower half of his body. A rear door of the car Carslake had borrowed specifically for this meeting opened and in slid Jake. He quickly shut out the weather.

"All a bit melodramatic, isn't it?" asked Jake. A gust hit the car, rocked it from side to side. The sky was black; rain on the way.

"Best no one is aware of this," replied Carslake. "I learned from experience long ago to take the better-safe-than-sorry approach right from the outset."

"Reculver, though. This place is the arse-end of beyond."

Windswept was an understatement when describing the tiny seaside hamlet half an hour's drive up the coast from the Ramsgate–Margate axis. Here, the buildings were set low to deal with whatever weather was thrown at them. Once, it had been a strategic location. The Roman fort, built two thousand years ago, on top of Iron Age defences, to guard the water channel before them, was just a grass-covered hump now. The only significant constructions were the pub and the twin towers of a ruined church slowly being consumed as the sea eroded the chalk cliff it stood above. Visitors were frequent here in the summer, when they could ride or walk the coastal path for uninterrupted mile upon mile. During an inclement spring they were, at best, rare.

"I'm sorry for your loss," said Carslake.

"Do you have any dead children?"

"No."

"Then you wouldn't have a clue what I'm going through and your apology is just words."

"I can empathise."

"I want your assistance, not your sympathy. How many years have I been paying you?"

"Don't." Carslake hated Jake shoving his corruption back into his face. He could just about live with himself otherwise, but Jake made it tough.

"What? You're bent." Jake leant forward, between the seats. "We're not friends together here. I give you money, you look out for me. If you're pissed off with me, I don't care. Get it?"

"Yes."

Jake sat back. "I had to learn about Regan from Solomon Gray, of all people."

"I couldn't warn you. The death knock had to be news."

Jake ground his teeth. "My dead son, *news*. It's all over social media. Even bloody William Noble is tweeting about Regan. I bet he's loving this."

"It's the way the world works now."

"Tell me the rest."

"Are you sure you want to hear?"

"Just get on with it."

Carslake adjusted his posture. He pulled his jacket tighter about him. It was cold. "Not much to say until after the post mortem tomorrow."

"I want the report as soon as it's available."

"You'll get it."

Carslake explained what he knew about the case, to date. When he'd finished, Jake sat for a few moments, thinking.

"Something smells," said Jake. "Regan out at sea; it doesn't make sense. There was no need for him to be taking on a sideline. My business is healthy, and he had plenty of folding money to play with."

Carslake shrugged.

"I want you to start digging," said Jake.

"I already am. It's my job."

"No, I mean more than just getting reports to me. Investigating."

"You're making me sound like a proper policeman now." Carslake couldn't help but put the sarcasm into his tone. Jake didn't seem to notice.

"You've got resources; make sure they're directed where I need them. Call me with everything, no matter how small." Jake popped open the passenger door. Carslake watched as the initial scene reversed itself – Jake returning to his car and driving away.

When Jake had gone, Carslake got out of his car. He needed to clear his head. He crossed the car park, buffeted by the wind, heading for the derelict church. Inside, the breeze lessened, whistling through columns of brick and the windows where glass had once been. It sounded to Carslake as if someone familiar were speaking to him. Carslake stood still and listened.

"Why?" They said. *"Why?!"*

Carslake's heart hammered against his rib cage, his breathing quickened. It felt as if all the air had been sucked out of the space he stood in. "Tom? Is that you?" His voice shook.

"*Why?!*"

Maybe not Gray's boy, maybe it was the others. The ones he'd never met but had helped sully him forever. Something brushed across Carslake's face. It felt like somebody breathing on him. He backed up against the wall, twisting his head from side to side, trying to see into the shadows. He almost pissed himself there and then. The wind increased, plucking at his clothes. Carslake's scalp itched, as if someone were running their fingers through his hair.

Carslake fronted up, as he always did. Shouted at them, though there was no strength in his words. But the wailing grew until he could stand it no more. He turned and ran.

Thirteen

"Your tie isn't straight," Underwood said to Gray.

He shrugged. "I doubt they'll be that bothered. I'm not the star turn."

They stood in the front reception area of the station. A knot of reporters was outside, talking to each other or on phones. Earlier, from an upstairs window, he'd watched vans and cars arrive, disgorging the journalists.

Underwood checked her watch. "Time to go."

"Remember, you're here for moral support," whispered Hamson. She squeezed his arm and smiled. Gray nodded. He held the door open for her, as Underwood hadn't bothered, and they walked out.

There was the immediate click of photos being taken and shouted questions from the assembled men and women of the press.

Underwood held up her hands, then pushed them down as if she were squeezing the noise into a box too small to contain it. Gray noticed Noble at the back of the pack.

"Quiet down please, ladies and gentlemen," said Underwood. "DI Hamson will read out a brief statement. There will be no time for questions." Underwood waved Hamson on. Reporters held phones out to record her words, cameras clicked again.

"Earlier today, the body of a twenty-six-year-old local man, Regan Armitage, along with two currently unidentified males, was found on a beach between Broadstairs and Ramsgate. One of the unidentified males had been stabbed. Although the post mortem is yet to be carried out, it's likely he died from his wounds.

"We believe another person escaped the scene. A man was discovered hiding in a beach hut at Dumpton Gap, but he fled. This man may be able to provide vital information to aid our investigation and we are making an appeal to find him. Miss Underwood has a photo of him and will hand out copies."

"Is it true that you're currently investigating the murder of Regan Armitage?" asked someone, a female by the voice.

"The investigation is ongoing, and I cannot comment on operational specifics."

"Could this man you're trying to track down be the murderer?" asked the same person.

Underwood stepped in before Hamson could answer. "I said no questions at this time." Underwood glared at the offending reporter who appeared totally unaffected by her gaze.

Hamson headed back indoors.

Noble appeared at Gray's side. Gray got a waft of Chinese food – Noble's offices were above a takeaway in the New Town area of Margate, a five-minute walk away.

"She's hardly endearing herself to my colleagues," said Noble.

"That's a common trait in Miss Underwood," said Gray.

Noble pouted. "This could have been my exclusive if you'd have just bent the rules a little."

"I'd bet a day's pay you put the story out anyway."

"It would be a disservice to my profession if I lied, therefore I will maintain a stoic silence."

"Which would make a change, Will."

"Anyway, all this is small beer compared to the other stuff I'm working on. When it comes out..." Noble shook his head. "Turmoil. Your lot will be really busy clearing up the mess."

"What mess?"

"Scoop of the century, Sol. So I'm keeping that one to myself. You'll know when it happens. Besides, you have dubious friends."

"Who?"

"See you around."

Noble turned and walked away, lost in the mix of bodies and leaving Gray with more unanswered questions.

Fourteen

Now that night had fallen, Khoury felt he could move around the town a little easier. The loss still burned in his heart. He was making his way back to the Lighthouse Project, the place his dreadlocked benefactor had pointed out to him earlier, only a few minutes from the shop where Khoury had acquired his new belongings. The polluted illumination of Dreamland was in front of him and beyond it the high rise of Arlington House bullied the skyline. A few lights twinkled from behind curtains.

As had become a habit, Khoury glanced over his shoulder. The pavement was empty except for the orange cast of intermittent sodium lamps. A fox paused as it crossed the road, spotting Khoury. When car headlights came around the corner, the animal burst into motion and was quickly lost to sight. As the vehicle passed by, Khoury turned his face away. The car drove on without slowing.

The building he wanted was a white-washed house in a terraced row identical to its neighbours except for the sign above the door which stated "Lighthouse Project Outreach Centre". Beside the words was a depiction of a lighthouse. Beneath the title was a strapline, "Shining out a light for the homeless". A yellow glow spilled out from the front door like its own beacon.

Steps reached up to the front door from the pavement. Khoury walked up them and entered. Within was a hall and a couple of doorways, ahead and to the right. The walls were plain; the floor varnished boards. Khoury glanced inside the nearest room. It was a reception area where a young woman, wearing faded denim dungarees, stood. Her dark hair was tied back. She had a name printed on a badge pinned to her chest which said "Rachel". She was heavily pregnant.

"Hello," she said, bright and alert.

Khoury didn't reply. Words didn't matter.

Rachel smiled. "We don't bite, and there's no need to tell me anything unless you want to. Including your name."

Khoury remained mute.

"Do you understand me?"

He nodded.

"We offer a bed for the night or there's hot food or both, depending on your preference. You can take a shower too or a bath. We don't want any trouble so no drug taking on site and no fighting. If either rule is broken, you'll be asked to leave. Did you understand all that?"

Khoury nodded again.

"Good. I'm Rachel." She tapped her badge. "Come find me if you need anything. Here's a blanket and a towel. Go back the way you came, turn right along the corridor, and you'll find everything out there."

"Okay."

Rachel grinned this time.

Khoury took the bedding, turned around, and followed his feet. Out the back, he entered a larger-than-expected room with rows of benches aligned vertically. To the rear was a long table at ninety degrees to the benches, covered with a plastic sheet. On top was a large urn, a pile of paper bowls, and plastic spoons. Behind the tables were a young man and a grey-haired woman, also wearing badges. *Kelvin. Natalie.* The smell issuing from the urn made Khoury's stomach lurch into life.

Khoury went further inside. Off to one side was another area with rows of beds, half of them filled with snoring people. To the other was a small kitchen area. He made his way over to the table.

"Vegetable soup," said Kelvin. "Would you like some?"

"Yes." Khoury kept his head down, not making eye contact with Kelvin or the woman.

Kelvin picked up a paper bowl and ladled a couple of dollops of soup in before handing it to Khoury. Natalie passed over a plastic spoon and a serviette. Khoury carried the bowl over to a table, put down the towel and sat. He poured some water from a jug into a plastic cup, took a sip. The water was tepid.

He turned his attention to the soup. Purely out of habit, Khoury dug around with the spoon first, searching for anything which shouldn't be there. Then he ate, his hunger overcoming his trust issues. It was decent enough, warm and filled with chunks of root vegetables. As soon as the first mouthful hit his stomach, he realised quite how hungry he was and devoured the lot, head low as possible over the food and shovelling it in at speed. When finished, he was back, holding out the bowl for Kelvin. Only partway through his third helping did Khoury's appetite began to sate.

Finally satiated, Khoury sat back. He considered having a shower. However, he realised he wasn't alone at the table. That in itself wouldn't be unusual, this was a hostel, after all, but the two other men were focused solely on him. They sat on either side a couple of feet away. Once they had Khoury's attention they shifted along to fill the gap so Khoury was hemmed in.

"Hungry little boy, aren't we?" said the first man. He had a beard, bad teeth, and one milky eye. The other, also bearded, with long, straggly hair stayed silent, glaring.

During his travel across Europe Khoury had learned to sense when trouble was near. This time his instincts had failed him. The air was thick with menace. Kelvin and Natalie were tending to the lengthening queue of homeless people. Khoury had to deal with this but not back down. He remembered Rachel's no fighting rule. It wouldn't do to be ejected.

"You're new here." The man with the milky eye stated the obvious. "Where are you from?"

Khoury said nothing.

One Eye smiled. "Don't matter if you speak or not, we can tell you're foreign just by looking at you. Ain't that right, Jez?"

Jez nodded stiffly.

"Let me tell you how it's going to be, my friend," continued One Eye. "You can stay here tonight. Get your head down, your belly full. We're not total bastards. But tomorrow, you move on, you don't come back. This place isn't for your type. Understand?"

"Is everything all right?" It was Natalie, from the food queue. She was standing right behind them. She was older than Rachel, her hair tied up in a similar fashion. She wore dungarees too.

"Everything's fine, little lady," said One Eye with a huge grin. "Just getting to know our new friend here."

Natalie visibly bristled. "Two things, Mr Hardwick. It's Natalie or Miss Peace, not *little lady* or any other derogatory term you may wish to use. Secondly, you know the rules. Any abuse or violence will result in you losing access to the hostel. Based on your past behaviour that would be for a week, again. Do you remember?"

"Yes."

"I'm glad we understand each other. Enjoy your evening." Natalie smiled sweetly and headed back over to the food bar.

"Bitch," muttered Hardwick under his breath. He turned back to Khoury. "Where were we in our little chat before her rude interruption? Oh yes, me telling you how it will be. The thing is, my friend, you and yours are a problem. A big, never-ending one. There are too many of you. Services are stretched, meaning less for the rest of us. If we keep letting everyone in, there'll be no space left. We were born here, you're an incomer. Understand?"

Khoury nodded. In his country, Khoury's attitude would be to eat Hardwick for lunch before Hardwick ate Khoury for dinner. But Khoury couldn't get the first blow in; he needed somewhere to sleep tonight so he had to let it go.

Hardwick patted Khoury on the face, said, "Good boy. I knew you were bright. There's a place more suited for your kind across town. The old Nayland Rock Hotel, you can't miss it. Go there tomorrow."

"Okay."

"Just in case you have second thoughts though: if you use this place again, I'll break your legs. Okay?"

Hardwick stood and left, trailed by Jez.

"Lights out in fifteen minutes," said Natalie.

Khoury made his way to the sleeping area. There were ten rows of cots, laid out close to each other, a narrow channel down the centre. Most were filled already with snoring men. A few men sat and talked together in low voices, pausing for a moment to eye Khoury before they returned to their conversation. A huge fart rent the air from someone over to his right.

There was a free cot against the far wall. He walked through the sleeping men. They were all white. No wonder he'd been targeted by Hardwick. Khoury lay down, removing only his boots, and wrapped himself up in a blanket. Back to the wall and facing the room. Eventually, if he was lucky, he might fall into a restless sleep.

Fifteen

Gray grabbed a beer from the fridge and his laptop from a bag, dragged open the floor-to-ceiling French window onto the balcony, and sat in the solitary wooden seat.

For a moment, he thought about what Carslake had told him. Had Tom really been taken to Europe? If so, why? Where the hell was he now? The trouble was, Gray was powerless. In the UK, at least Gray could have spoken to colleagues. They would probably have helped a fellow officer, even if they hadn't known each other. But in a foreign country? And in a foreign language? The challenge was immense, but the new lead was huge. For the first time in ages he had a path to follow.

Gray had settled into his new home faster than he'd expected. Perhaps it was the view; the uninterrupted seascape as far as the eye could see across almost one-hundred-and-eighty degrees of panorama. Perhaps it was the lack of garden to deal with – not a single piece of greenery – or that there weren't any families around him anymore, reminding of what he didn't have. Or maybe it was leaving the past behind. Ultimately, it didn't matter what the cause was as long as the effect was acceptable. Other than Carslake and Hamson, he'd had no visitors since he'd moved in a month ago.

High panels either side of the balcony blocked him off from the neighbours. The upstairs balcony overhung, providing an element of shade on the sunniest of days. Below was the clifftop walkway to Viking Bay; beneath that, the sand and surf of Louisa Bay.

The location was as good as it got and the cost of the flat was accordingly high. Gray's finances had stretched sufficiently because his old house was within the catchment area of the best local schools, a feature that parents were desperate to pay for and that estate agents ruthlessly promoted. In fact, two families had entered a bidding war to acquire his property. Gray had ended up getting ten thousand pounds over the asking price. So, although Gray had a mortgage again, it was manageable.

Also manageable was the beer, which disappeared far too easily, bottle empty before he realised. Once it was gone however, it was gone. His was a new start. While packing for the move, Gray had poured all the spirits down the drain. He'd scrunched up the final pack of cigarettes, a couple unsmoked.

Since then he'd been attempting no more than one beer and two coffees a day. He was exercising a little too, jogging on a treadmill in the spare bedroom, though he wasn't yet at the point where he felt confident enough to go out on the street in plain view.

He missed the pub, the experience of enjoying a beer. He'd tried orange juice a couple of times, but it wasn't the same. Boozers were for boozing in.

And for all the supposed benefits of taking up a healthier lifestyle, Gray sometimes felt unwell. The odd bout of constipation, an upset stomach from certain foods, a transgression as Hamson had pointed out. Gray put it down to irritable bowel syndrome as his body grumbled adjusting to his change in diet. Nothing disabling, more of an irritant. Being sick was new, though. And the food sticking in his throat.

Gray dismissed the symptoms; they'd pass. He clicked the Facebook icon on his laptop. He'd only recently set up an account. There were only two people he'd consider friends, Carslake and Hamson, and he saw them most days. He wasn't interested in connecting with other work colleagues or old school mates. There was a reason he'd drifted away from them and it would be staying that way. He'd joined Facebook because of his daughter, Hope.

Gray's current objective, however, was Regan. He found his profile immediately. The main photograph was of a grinning, slightly younger Regan, seemingly in a pub, someone's arm around his shoulders, the person's face cropped out. The banner photo was a wide angle shot of the club, Seagram's, lit up at night. Regan's personal data was innocuous. He'd labelled himself as single, born in Margate, worked at Enterprise Associated Partners, his father's company, his title of Director in capitals. The page's structure shouted success and good times.

Regan's timeline was awash with messages. A long scroll of posts unable to comprehend that Regan was gone, that he'd been taken too young, offering condolences to the family. Then quite a few who said good riddance to bad rubbish, and worse. Gray clicked on some of the friends who'd posted and took in their profile too. He couldn't believe how much information people dumped into the public domain.

A buzz from within the flat interrupted Gray's research. It was a call from the lobby. He picked up the entry phone.

"It's Jake. Can I come up?"

Surprised, Gray paused a moment before he told Jake his flat number. Gray went onto the balcony and shut down the laptop. A few minutes later there was a knock on the front door.

"This is unexpected," said Gray. "Come in."

Jake stepped inside and glanced around. "I didn't know who else to speak to."

"The Samaritans?"

"I'm depressed, not fucking suicidal, Sol. It's not in me."

Gray led Jake onto the balcony.

"Great view," said Jake, leaning on the railings.

"It's one of the reasons I bought it. Fancy a beer?"

"How about ten?"

Gray grabbed a couple of bottles from the fridge, breaking his own rule again, and popped the caps. He carried them back outside and handed one over to Jake who was still looking out to sea.

"Thanks." Jake accepted the bottle and took a deep draft.

"I'm sorry about Regan," said Gray.

"So, this is what it feels like."

"Yes." There wasn't anything Gray could say to make it better so he didn't.

"Remember when we were kids, Sol? Best mates."

Inseparable, thought Gray, but said, "Long time ago."

"That it is. They were good days."

"Different days."

"Before anything mattered."

And before we took our different paths.

"Now look at us," said Jake.

Again, Gray didn't know how to reply. He wasn't the best at eloquent, meaningful statements. He let the silence stretch.

Eventually Jake said, "How's the new place?"

"Fine. Does what it needs to."

"Better than rattling around in that old house of yours. Too many memories?"

"That was one problem." Another pause until Gray said, "I'm sure you didn't come over just to reminisce."

"You know me too well. I've a favour to ask."

"Okay."

"Will you come to the funeral?"

Gray groaned inside. He hadn't liked Regan very much. Going seemed hypocritical.

Peering at Gray, Jake said, "I don't hear a yes, Sol."

"I'm not sure I can."

"Why? Too *busy* to be at the side of an old friend?" Gray heard the disdain in his voice. "I'm sorry I asked." Jake rose.

"Wait." Gray put a hand on his arm. He was being utterly selfish. What he thought of Regan was of no importance here. "I'll be there."

"Thanks a lot, Sol, I really appreciate it."

"As you said, Jake. Old friends."

"And the wake afterwards? It'll be at Seagram's."

Which would mean getting drunk at the club. "That's a maybe."

"Okay, I can live with that." Jake drained the beer, said, "Any more of these?"

Gray had barely touched his. He got Jake another.

"I feel like I failed them you know, Sol. Let everybody down; everyone I've ever loved."

"We all fail in some way or another."

"I'm not sure which of us is worse. You losing your kid or me driving them away."

"Thanks, Jake, I appreciate that."

"I'm sorry; I didn't mean it that way. You know me; I'm a heart-on-sleeve kind of man. Sometimes what's up here," Jake tapped the bottle against his forehead, "falls out of my mouth with no moderation in between."

"It's not a problem."

"Look, I'll leave you to whatever." Jake was clearly embarrassed.

"Did you drive over?"

"I'm parked just round the corner."

"I'll call you a taxi then. Your car will be fine overnight. Then we can have another beer."

"It's okay, I'd better be off anyway."

Gray showed Jake to the door.

"See you at the funeral then?" asked Jake.

"Wouldn't miss it."

When Jake was gone, Gray returned to the balcony, sat down, and opened up his laptop once more. There were already additional messages on Regan's Facebook timeline. Gray skimmed them, but wasn't really paying attention. Jake's comment about failing his family was stuck in his mind.

Gray accessed the Facebook search function. He typed in "Hope Simpson". His daughter had taken her mother's maiden name some time ago. Gray knew Hope lived in Edinburgh; almost as far away from Kent as it was possible to get. She was nineteen now and partway through a nursing qualification at Napier University there.

It was the work of moments to find her Facebook profile, even though they weren't classified as friends. Her timeline contained plenty of smiling photographs with a wide array of people, none of which Gray recognised. Why would he? He wondered if one was a partner. Was she in a long-term relationship? How were her studies going? What did her voice sound like? It had been so long since they'd talked. Every time he'd gone to pick up the phone, his guilt had got the better of him, and he'd never made the call.

He'd read that people these days, particularly the young who'd grown up with social media as a constant, tended to project a face onto the world that didn't really exist. Gray hoped she was as happy as the photos suggested. He closed the laptop lid and the balcony darkened. A gull, riding the thermals, flitted past. The bloody things never seemed to sleep.

Gray's phone vibrated on the table top. Noble again. Gray rejected the call twice, though each time the ring tone kicked in immediately. Then a text bleeped: "HELP".

When Noble called again Gray answered. "Bit melodramatic this evening, Will."

All he received in reply was a groan and a drawn-out cough.

"Will? Will, are you okay? What's going on?"

All he got was another groan. He left his flat at a run, slamming the door behind him. He took the stairs, rather than wait for the lift to arrive, jumped into his car, and drove as fast as he was able to Noble's Margate office.

Sixteen

Despite a chorus of snores, Khoury slept fitfully in the crowded room. He dreamt he was in the sea, far from shore. His arms were useless. He couldn't stay afloat any longer, no matter how hard he fought. Khoury sank beneath the waves, his lungs filling with water as the light receded.

He awoke with a jerk, breathing heavily. It was dark, but he didn't think he'd been asleep long; no more than an hour, maybe less. He sat up, unsure of his surroundings. Then he recalled he was in the homeless shelter in a strange country. His family were dead. His friends were dead. The irony of it all. He, Najjar and Shadid had survived years of civil war in Syria, only to die at the hands of their "rescuer". His wife and child had perished in a place where they were supposed to be safe. Khoury lay back down and stared at the ceiling.

Yesterday, he and his two friends thought they'd finally found a way to England from France. He recalled the man's words: *A short trip on a fishing boat, and you're free.* Remarkably straightforward after such an arduous route from Syria, followed by months stuck in a squalid camp in Calais. Khoury looked forward to the day they were settled because then his wife could travel over from Syria, and they'd finally be a family again. How long had it been since he'd comforted his daughter when she woke from a bad dream? But once on the waves, it had all gone wrong. The drowning of the white man, and the stabbing of his brother Najjar with Najjar's own knife. With the memory, fury flared within him once more. He'd felt fear and anger when his neighbourhood had been bombed to ruin, but this was different. This betrayal was personal.

Khoury didn't know what had happened to Shadid. He'd glimpsed him cowering beside the bulkhead before Khoury threw himself overboard. Khoury floated momentarily, glimpsed the words Etna and Ramsgate on the stern before he began swimming and someone began shouting.

Somehow, what seemed like hours later, Khoury made it ashore. Half in, half out of the surf, he had retched. It took a few minutes for him to regain his breath. He began to shiver. He was drained, every muscle ached, his throat sore from gulping down seawater when a wave had caught him. He breathed deeply, taking air into his straining lungs. He had to move, it wasn't safe here. But he stood for a moment, water dripping off him. His clothes were sodden, the fabric cold against his skin. He shivered in the night air.

In the moonlight, he'd been able to see a white cliff before him, sand and rock all around. There was a faint twinkle of lights, which meant people, so he decided to head that way.

After stumbling along for ten minutes or so, Khoury reached a concrete esplanade and a few small wooden huts. Were these tiny homes? Did people live here? They all looked shuttered. He needed somewhere to dry himself; somewhere to sleep that was out of the way. He expected the men from the boat would come looking for him. In a way, that's what he wanted, because, as they said back home, one who cooks poison should taste it. But, at the moment, he wasn't ready. Too wet, weak, too cold.

All the huts were fastened up tight, so Khoury collected a heavy rock from the beach below. As he swung the rock at the first of the two locks on the door, it slipped out of his frozen fingers. Shivering, he picked up the stone and tried again, this time catching the metal hard enough to rip the screws out of the wood. When he was done, he tossed the shattered catches away, shot the bolts, swung back the door, and peered within.

In the moonlight, he saw the interior was a surprisingly neat space. A bench along the back with a curtain hanging below, shelves on either wall, hooks for towels, various beach paraphernalia and toys, stuff for toddlers. He spotted a set of toddler swim wings and flashed back to his little girl's first time in the water. Laila, his daughter. Laila, Shadid's niece. She'd flapped her little arms, giggling "Baba! Baba!" as she splashed him. Overhead was a lantern which he switched on, then pulled the doors closed behind him.

In the dim glow, Khoury undertook a more thorough search. He found towels and a hoodie, which appeared a bit small, though would have to do. He discarded his wet shirt, vigorously towelled himself dry and dragged on the too-tight top. If he tugged at the sleeves to stretch them they just about ran to his wrists. He took a knife out of his pocket, put it on the floor, then pulled off his trousers and dried his legs. Finally, he hung a couple of towels over his shoulders for additional warmth.

But he couldn't be a beggar acting like a rich man. A beggar was what he'd become during his transit across Europe. No longer a teacher who helped others; now someone who lived by their good or ill. Usually the latter.

A kettle sat on a portable burner and, next to it, coffee, tea, sugar, and, mercifully, a plastic bottle half full of water. It could be days old, but he didn't care. Khoury poured what there was into the kettle and lit the gas.

He threw granules into a mug, added a couple of spoonfuls of sugar for a sliver of energy and poured hot water on top. There was half a packet of biscuits in a makeshift bin. They were soft. Khoury didn't care. He sat on the floor, drew the towels tighter around him, and held the hot mug in his hands to warm them up. When he felt warmer, he ate the biscuits which crumbled at a touch and drank the coffee. It was weak compared to what he was used to.

His first objective was to stay under the radar. He was sure the police would be looking for him. Perhaps they'd even consider him a suspect. Then he must seek revenge. He must find and kill the men who'd murdered one, and probably both, of his friends. Family honour dictated it. That was okay. He'd done it before in the name of civil liberty. Despite the coffee, Khoury felt the tiredness creep over him. He'd expended a lot of energy getting himself ashore and his body was shutting down. He tried to fight it; he needed to move soon, before someone found him.

Khoury hadn't realised he'd fallen asleep until the latch rattled and a person, flanked by two children, stared down at him. All he could see was silhouettes, the rising sun behind them.

"Who's that man, Mummy?" asked one of the children, a girl by her voice. She appeared more curious than frightened. The woman, however, was hardly the model of calmness. She took a step forward, pushing the kids behind her, out of the way.

"Get out!" the woman shrieked at him.

Khoury leapt up, the knife in his hand. The woman, despite her initial bravado, moved backwards now, holding her children protectively. "Philip!" shouted the woman. A glance showed a man waddling down a slope from the cliff above, laden with bags, shuffling in flip flops.

Khoury grabbed his trousers and boots and began running, ignoring the stiffness from lying on a wooden floor. His dash took him past Philip, who slowly put down the bags and ran a few steps before halting.

"Hey!" said Philip. "Come back here!"

Khoury passed a boarded-up café and terraces of more permanent-looking, shuttered huts.

He rounded a corner, out of sight of the family. He paused to put on his trousers. Above him, a chalk cliff, studded with flint, towered. Below, the beach and the receding sea. The only obvious way up was the slope he'd seen Philip on, though he wasn't going back to it. He had no choice but to carry on and hope he discovered an escape route before the police arrived and he was trapped …

THE CLATTER OF METAL and a man's loud swearing ended Khoury's recollections and brought him back to the present. He turned his head and caught the sight of a dim beam of light on the floor. Somebody stooped, picked up a flashlight. Khoury watched the man shine the torch into the face of one comatose vagrant after another.

Part way along the row the man stopped, aimed the beam in a sleeper's face for a long moment, flicked the illumination over to a piece of paper he held in a fist, and back again. It was an easy assumption to make that it was a photo.

"Hey," whispered the torch man.

"What?" There was another figure working the far side of the room, the pair splitting the search between them.

"Check this guy out."

"Give me a moment." He made his way over, torch light downwards, stepping over stuff.

"What do you think?"

"It's not him."

"Are you sure? It looks like him."

"Definitely not."

"What makes you so sure?"

"Because he's white. We're looking for coloured skin."

"Could be a tan."

The first guy groaned. "Christ, I wish this was over. These guys stink. Makes me want to slap one of them."

This time the beam was directed into the face of the first searcher, illuminating a shaven, bullet-shaped head. Khoury recognised him immediately from the boat. He knocked the hand down so the light was no longer in his eyes.

"Stop whining, Dave. I don't want to be here anymore than you, so let's get it done quick, okay?"

"Don't tell me what to do, Larry." The menace was clear in Dave's voice.

Khoury grimaced in the darkness. They were here for him. They'd come to him. Khoury couldn't believe his luck. The pair split up again and methodically worked their way through the hostel guests. They were being thorough, checking everyone, working from opposite ends and concluding in the centre before repeating the process. Twice more they paused, checked the photo against a face, moved on.

Row four became three. If he'd been sleeping near the door the pair would have found him by now. Fight or flight? Khoury decided on flight for now. They were big men; Khoury didn't think he could take both. He worked best by stealth. He'd bide his time.

The only escape route was to leap out of bed and jump over the sleepers in his way. If the pair were slow to react, perhaps he could make it. Outside, he could decide whether to keep running or follow them, depending on circumstances. Khoury tensed, ready to leap. He slowly peeled the covers back, but before he could move, the overhead light flicked on. Khoury dropped onto the floor, to remain hidden now the room was illuminated.

"What are you doing?" Rachel was standing in the doorway.

"We're looking for a friend," said Larry as he switched off his torch. "He's disappeared, and we're worried about him."

Dave, a black man with long dreadlocks, stayed quiet.

"You're not allowed back here," said Rachel.

"We were told it was okay."

"By who?"

"Your colleague."

"Kelvin?"

"That's him."

"Well, he was wrong to say so. What's your friend's name? The one you're looking for."

"Wayne?"

"You don't sound sure."

"It's definitely Wayne."

"Is that a photo?" Rachel pointed at the paper in Larry's fingers. She held out her hand. "Can I take a look? I may recognise him."

Reluctantly, Larry passed over the photo. Rachel glanced at it, shook her head. "This person looks Arabic."

"So?"

"Wayne isn't a very common Arabic name."

"Are you taking the piss?"

"It's not me who's taking the piss. I can tell you this man hasn't come in here tonight."

"You know all of them then?" The mockery in Larry's voice was clear.

"Pretty much. I was on the front desk, so everyone came past me and most of our guests are regulars. So, yes, I'd know. And this man is not in here."

"Your friend, Kelvin, says he is. Served him food earlier."

Rachel shrugged, unaffected. "Kelvin's new. Faces look similar at first. He made a mistake."

Larry wouldn't be deterred. "I want to see them all."

Rachel shook her head. "As I said, that's not possible."

Larry stepped in, got right up to Rachel's face. "Get the fuck out our way, now! Or I'll do something you'll regret!" He raised his hand in a fist.

Rachel stood her ground, crossing her arms above her protruding belly, though her face paled. "You'd hit a pregnant woman."

"Happily."

"In front of all these witnesses?" Rachel pointed past Larry. Some of the men in the room were awake and sitting up, watching proceedings.

"Yes, hello, I need the police please." Khoury recognised the voice. It was the older woman, Natalie. She entered the room, a phone pressed to her ear. "A disturbance at the Lighthouse Project."

Larry grabbed the phone from Natalie's grasp, ended the call.

"You'd better go," said Natalie. "The police will be here in a minute. They're only around the corner and know to come quickly when there's trouble."

Dave put an arm out, said, "Larry, mate, let's be off."

Larry shook the restraining hand away, tossed the phone on the floor, and stalked out, Dave in his tracks. Rachel apologised for disturbing everyone's sleep, but most were already unconscious again. As altercations went, it was minor. No punches had been thrown. Natalie and Rachel followed the two men, presumably to ensure they did actually leave.

Khoury slipped his boots on, rose, and went into the eating area. Only Rachel was there, one hand on her head, the other on her belly. She looked startled when she saw Khoury.

"Can I see?" asked Khoury.

She passed over the piece of paper. It was a photo of him, not great quality but clear enough to be recognisable. Khoury scrunched the paper up into a ball and dropped it onto the floor.

"We can help," said Rachel.

Khoury shook his head. He could only help himself, the way it always had been. He returned to his bed, collected his coat, and pulled out the knife. Back in the refectory, Rachel looked down at the blade, then back up to Khoury. She stepped backwards.

Khoury pushed past Rachel, making her stumble. *Where had the two men gone?* He rushed for the front of the house. Natalie was on the pavement, arguing with Larry. He was standing beside a car, the passenger door open, engine idling.

"Leave," she said. "Before the police get here. We'll talk later."

Larry looked like he had something else to say, but he got inside the car, and it was moving before he had the door closed. Khoury dashed down the steps, but the car was going too fast for him.

Khoury took a couple of steps back towards Natalie. He wanted to know more about Larry, this man who had probably killed his friends. Clearly, Natalie knew something, knew Larry. But he heard a siren. Blue flashing lights rounded the corner from the seafront. Khoury turned and dashed in the opposite direction, anger blooming.

Close – he'd been so close. He knew where to start looking now, though. He'd be back. For Natalie.

Seventeen

The office of *Thanet's Voice* was in Margate's New Town, above a Chinese takeaway in the pedestrianised shopping area. The entrance was down an alley, a black door behind two large blue bins on wheels. A large extractor fan blew hot air. The alley reeked of stale food and piss.

The door yawned open. Immediately inside was dimness and a set of stairs. Gray fumbled around until he felt a light switch and flicked it on. Noble was lying face down at the top of the stairs, his head and one arm hanging over the uppermost step. It didn't look good for him. Noble's face was covered in blood, one eye swollen.

Gray ran up and knelt down beside him. He put his ear next to Noble's mouth. His breath washed in and out. Gray was hugely relieved.

"Will, it's me, Sol. I'm here."

Noble's only reply was a groan.

"I'll call you an ambulance. Hang on."

Gray picked up Noble's phone from where it had fallen from his hand and dialled 999. He gave Noble's torso a quick check over. Noble groaned when Gray felt his chest. Maybe a cracked rib? It looked like he'd taken a good kicking from someone. Gray decided it wasn't wise to move Noble into the recovery position. Doing so might make things worse. Next,

Gray called the station and asked for some uniforms to be sent down.

Satisfied he couldn't do any more for Noble, Gray took a quick look around. There were three doorways off the landing. Directly behind Noble was the office. It was a mess. Paper strewn everywhere. Drawers dragged out, files all over the floor. An assault on Noble and a hasty search for something. But what?

When Gray went back onto the landing to check on Noble again he found him leaning upright against the wall, his eyes closed.

"Stay where you are," said Gray. He crouched; put a hand on Noble's shoulder. "The ambulance will be here in a few minutes."

"I'm all right." Noble pushed Gray weakly away. "I don't need anyone." Noble ruined his own diagnosis by leaning over and vomiting down the stairs. When there was no more to throw up, Noble sat back up again, wiped his mouth, and grinned weakly. "Okay, maybe I do. They didn't find it, though."

"Find what?"

"Hello?" A call from the bottom of the stairs. "Ambulance." Two paramedics at the bottom of the stairs.

"Here," said Gray, standing.

Gray moved out of the way to allow the paramedics access to Noble.

"Nothing major," said one to Gray after they'd given Noble a quick check over, "but we'll take him to the hospital, just to be sure."

Noble crooked a finger at Gray. "We need to talk."

"When you're better."

"Tomorrow," said Noble. "I'll call you."

Uniform arrived then; two constables.

"You took your time," said Gray.

"Sorry, sir, there's an incident at the Lighthouse Project."

The constables shifted to one side while the paramedics helped Noble to his feet and supported him during the descent. Gray followed. Then the medics put Noble on a stretcher and loaded him into the back of the ambulance. The doors closed and the ambulance drove away, watched by a couple of faces standing in the takeaway's window.

"Come with me," said Gray to the DCs. He entered the takeaway. The odour of Chinese food was much stronger inside, the smell always reminded Gray of sweet and sour sauce, the red stuff that quickly congealed on balls of an unidentified meat surrounded by a light golden batter. The crackle of hot oil in a pan and the scraping of metal on metal as an unseen chef in the back cooked was the only sound. Three men stood in the narrow space between the door and the metal-topped counter. They stared sullenly at Gray. A white carrier bag rested on the metal surface. From the shape of it there was clearly a takeaway within.

Behind the counter, a large, handwritten menu was nailed to the wall. Beneath it, a short Asian woman wearing an apron blinked at Gray through thick glasses. She'd been trying to disappear out the doorway into the kitchen but stopped now. As if Gray would only see her if she moved.

He showed his warrant card and said, "A man has just been assaulted. Did any of you see anything?" He received blank looks in return from all.

"Somebody must have seen something," said Gray. Still nobody offered a response. "Right, I'll be taking you all down the station for further questioning." Gray turned his attention to the woman. "You'll have to close down for the night."

"Fuck's sake, mate, what about my food?" The man who'd spoken appeared the youngest of the three. He wore black leather, and his bottom lip was pierced with a small silver ring. He pointed his thumb at the carrier bag. "It'll go cold."

"Tell me what you saw. Then you can go."

"All I saw was you walk past, then the ambulance and cops arrive."

"That's it?"

"Yeah. None of us have been here long. It's a takeaway. Fast food, you know? Maybe it was you who beat up that bloke?"

The man glared at Gray. "Give your name and contact details to my colleagues here; then you can be on your way, all of you."

Gray turned to the Chinese woman. "Did you see anything?" She shook her head. "Do you know the man who lives above?"

"No."

"Nobody walked past? You didn't hear any noises from above."

He got a shrug in reply then, "You all look same to me."

Eighteen

Dr Ben Clough's hands always felt cold. After every time they shook hands, Gray had to fight the urge to rub his own together to warm them up again. He couldn't figure out if it was a genetic thing with Clough or whether it was because he spent the majority of his time in the mortuary where the temperature was kept permanently low.

Clough was the silent, considerate type. He was a runner – another solitary pastime – pounding the streets out of hours. At some point, Gray would ask his advice on the mundane matter of exercise, though at a more appropriate time.

Gray had driven over to the hospital, rather than head into the station, setting off before the beginning of his shift in order to beat the traffic. Thanet was a maze of indirect, restricted routes which had a tendency to bottleneck at the slightest opportunity, making the journey half an hour rather than ten minutes. Clough was an early starter, too.

The pair sat in the pathologist's tiny, airless office. A desk, a couple of chairs, a pair of filing cabinets, and it was full.

"I made a start as soon as I could," said Clough. "I thought it prudent."

"Fine with me." Gray didn't like watching a corpse being dissected. "Any revelations?"

"Best I show you."

Clough led Gray to the storage area. The air was several degrees cooler, and Gray could see his breath fog. There were many small metal doors set into the wall in rows, floor to ceiling. Clough undid the latch on one at waist height. Cold spilled out, and Gray shivered involuntarily. The pathologist tugged on the gurney inside and Regan's shrouded corpse was silently revealed, the bed moving on well-oiled runners.

Clough lifted one corner of the white sheet to expose a wrist, leaving the rest of the body hidden. Gray bent closer to see what Clough was pointing to.

"Abrasions," said Gray.

"Correct. And not just there." Clough moved down the body, lifted back the adjacent corner, bringing a leg into view. "It's the same on both wrists and ankles."

"He was bound hand and foot?"

Clough nodded. "And these." He folded back the sheet, keeping Regan's face and half his body covered. There was bruising on the side of his ribcage, the marks livid.

"He was assaulted, probably kicked. By the arrangement of the discoloration I'd suggest he curled up into a ball to protect himself."

"Cause of death was drowning?"

"His lungs were inundated with liquid, if that's what you mean."

"So, he drowned then, Ben."

"You know how the process works?"

"They breathe water rather than air, which isn't particularly good for them."

"Very droll, but basically correct. The fluid obstructs the airway which causes asphyxia. Circulatory and respiratory failure occurs almost immediately."

"Nice."

"Quite. To be honest, it's usually difficult to conclusively establish death by drowning. The lungs naturally fill if a corpse is submerged for any reasonable time, meaning the findings in any investigation are at best minimal."

"Really?"

"Surprisingly, yes. There's several signs to look out for." Clough held a hand up in a fist. Gray was about to get a lesson. "One, a white froth at the nose and mouth." Clough extended a finger. "But there was none. Possibly washed away in the surf. Two, the presence of weeds or stones grasped by the hands. Desperation at the nearing end. There were none — perhaps nothing could be grabbed? Three, foam in the lungs and air passage, which was present. Four, water-logged lungs, also a check, though as I've already said that's entirely natural. Five, water in the stomach and intestines, ditto." Clough raised his other hand in a fist. "Six, diatoms and maybe plankton in the tissues."

Gray opened his mouth to ask the obvious question. Clough got there first.

"They're algae found in water and they're what can prove the evidence we need. The diatoms pass from the ruptured alveolar wall into lymph channels and pulmonary veins and then into the heart. Only a live body with circulation can transport diatoms from the water into organs in that fashion."

"The heart pumping junk around the body?"

"Right. No pump, no diatoms where they shouldn't be."

"Bloody hell, Ben, are you going to tell me if you saw them or continue being far too clever for your own good?"

"Sorry, I get a bit carried away."

Gray felt like screaming.

"Yes, there were diatoms."

"And time of death?"

"Again, difficult to establish because of the body's time in the sea. It's effectively a huge heat sink. Could have been hours or days. Given the preserved nature of the cadaver I'd tend towards the former – limited time as fish food," clarified Clough. "It's usually the eyes that get eaten first. I also took a blood sample for analysis. Because I knew you'd be in a hurry I called in a favour, walked the sample over, stuck around and made a general nuisance of myself until I got the data." Clough handed over a file. He did enjoy a degree of melodrama.

In this case it was warranted.

"Ketamine," said Gray.

Clough nodded. "Enough to knock him out and make him compliant. Regan ingested the drug at some point prior to his immersion. And being in a relative state of helplessness would in all likelihood actively reduce the signs of drowning."

"What about the other two?"

"I've yet to undertake the full post mortems. Outward appearances signpost similar drowning indicators to Regan in one. The knife wound in the other may or may not have been fatal. I won't know for sure until I go inside later today." Clough held up a hand; palm towards Gray. "And yes, before you ask, I've sent their blood samples away too, although I'm afraid you'll have to wait for those. I can only work one miracle at a time."

"That'll do me, Ben."

They shook hands once more. When Clough was out of sight Gray rubbed his palms together and only stopped to answer his phone. He checked the display. Hamson.

"Are you still at the hospital?" she asked.

"Yes, why?"

"We had a report of a disturbance last night at the Lighthouse Project on Belgrave Road. Seems like our mystery man was there."

"Okay, I'm on my way."

"Not yet. There's a witness in the hospital you should speak to, if you can. Rachel O'Shea."

Nineteen

Then

It was the fire engine which brought Rachel back to the here and now. She withdrew from Cameron's clinch.

"What's wrong?" he asked.

They sat side by side with their feet dangling over the water. Below her, the waves lapped at the Harbour Arm wall. Nearby, a couple of boats bobbed on the calm water of the anchorage. She preferred it when the sea was up and wild. When spray was in the air and there was the crackle of an impending storm. Tonight, though, everything was still.

The fire engine raced along the Margate sea front, blue lights briefly lost among the permanently lit, lurid display of Dreamland. The sirens wailed, even though there was no queue of cars to shunt out of the way. Rachel returned her attention to Cameron. It would be someone else's tragedy; she couldn't help.

When the second engine and a police car went in the same direction, Rachel broke off from Cameron again. She ignored his protests. The red stain of a blaze was clear on the black sky. She jolted inside when she realised the first fire engine had stopped near where she was staying.

She jumped up and ran as fast as she could, Cameron close behind her. She ignored his shouted questions. By the time she arrived, both fire engines were spraying water on the building.

She paused, took in the sight: fire licking out of the first-floor windows, smoke billowing. The heat increased as she neared. She could feel it on her skin, a warm caress. A small crowd had gathered, watching behind a cordon, powerless to intervene. She ran over, couldn't see her family there. She ducked under the tape and dashed to the burning house.

A policeman grabbed her round the waist before she'd advanced two feet. She struggled. He tried to calm her.

"My father and brother are in there!" she shouted.

"You need to stay back!"

The policeman let go, and Rachel fell into Cameron's arms. A man wearing a crumpled suit came over. He was also police, he said. There was a bright flash, then another. Someone taking photos. The policeman left Rachel and Cameron with his colleague, whose name was Jeff, and went to talk to the cameraman.

Jeff led Rachel to the sea wall and made her sit down. She held Cameron's hand. The concrete was cold beneath her. Jeff took off his jacket which smelt faintly of smoke, and draped it around her shoulders.

The three of them watched the fire burn.

Twenty

Now Gray was directed by a nurse to a private room off one of the many wards. Gray knocked lightly on the door.

"Come in," said someone from inside.

He entered, closing the door behind him. Inside was the patient, a pregnant woman who lay on her back, seemingly asleep, dark hair spread across the pillow. Some monitors beside the bed bleeped intermittently. There was a bunch of flowers standing on the windowsill in a vase. Lilies. Beautiful to look at, not so great to smell. As if something had died and was in the process of rotting. Hardly ideal for a hospital environment of recovery and recuperation.

A grey-haired woman sat in a chair drawn up to the bed. A newspaper lay in her lap, and she was regarding Gray expectantly.

"I'm looking for Rachel O'Shea," said Gray.

"She's asleep," said the woman, standing.

Gray introduced himself, showed his warrant card.

"May I?" Natalie held out a hand. Gray passed over his card. She examined it closely before handing it back. "I'm Natalie Peace. Rachel and I work together."

"How is she?"

"Let's talk outside. I read somewhere that unconscious people can hear conversations." Natalie tucked the newspaper under an arm.

Just along the corridor was a small, square recess with seats bolted to the floor and a vending machine which Natalie fed some coins into. "Would you like something?" she asked.

He shook his head. Natalie pushed several times at the keypad, making a selection, and waited for the machine to dispense a drink. A few moments later, she held a small plastic cup in her hands, blowing on the surface, although Gray couldn't see any steam rising. She took a sip and pulled a face.

"What do you want?" said Natalie.

"My boss called and told me to speak to you. She said Miss O'Shea was involved in an altercation with a man, possibly a person of interest in a case we're investigating."

"I'm the manager of the Lighthouse Project on Belgrave Road. We provide a refuge for the homeless. Rachel is a volunteer."

"I know it. Not the easiest of places to work, I imagine."

"Sometimes, no. But I enjoy it."

"It's under threat though?"

Natalie scowled. "Bloody developers are after us, yes."

"Have you had any trouble previously?"

"There's sometimes a few scrapes, it's the nature of the beast. But nothing like this."

"What happened?"

"Two men came in, looking for someone. Rachel discovered them out the back in the dormitory, shining a torch into the faces of sleeping guests."

"How did they gain access?"

"Kelvin let them in."

"Who's he?"

"Another volunteer. If we weren't short of people I'd get rid of him." An angry expression crossed her face. "The fact is they shouldn't have been there. It's against the rules."

"Why?"

"We try to provide a safe and secure environment for our sleepers. It's tough out on the streets."

"What time did this happen, precisely?"

"Just after 1am."

"Did you know them?"

She shook her head.

"Can you describe them?"

"Locals, by their accents. Big guys, not pleasant at all. Not homeless by how they were dressed; too smart and they wore aftershave."

"You were brave to stand up to them."

"It was Rachel, really. I just called your lot. You get used to dealing with difficult people and situations. They weren't pleased. I followed them outside to ensure they left."

"Does this happen very often? Someone trying to find people?"

"Yes, unfortunately. Usually family members looking for a runaway. But they've left home for a reason and don't want to be located. It's our job to be impartial."

"How did Rachel end up needing to be hospitalised?"

"I don't really know. I was outside when it all happened, showing the two men off the premises. One of our guests ran past me into the street and kept going. I went back in and found Rachel on the floor. Kelvin was looking after her. He'd already called an ambulance; the police came pretty much straight away. We've been in here ever since. The baby's all right though, thank God."

"What did the man look like? The one they were looking for."

Natalie passed Gray the newspaper. On the front page was a picture of their mystery man from the earlier press conference. "It was him. Look, I've got to get back in to Rachel. Is that everything you need to know?"

"What about the baby's father?"

"He's working. He'll be here soon. I really need to be with Rachel."

"Of course, I'm sorry I've kept you for so long. Thanks for your help. I'll send someone over to take a formal statement and show you some photos when you're feeling up to it. Perhaps you'll recognise the men." Gray handed over his business card. "In case you remember anything else."

Natalie put the plastic cup down on the table and left. When Gray walked passed Rachel's room the door was closed.

His phone beeped; a text message. It was from Noble. It said, "I'm out. Meet me later."

"Where and when?" tapped out Gray.

"Tonight English Flag."

Gray groaned. The place was a dump. But at least he might learn why Noble had been beaten.

Twenty One

Mike Fowler was like a cat, waiting to pounce the moment Gray sat down. He dropped a file in front of Gray.

"French police have responded," said Fowler, almost purring, leaning over Gray's desk. "We've got a name for our mystery man. Adnan Khoury. And they've identified the other corpses too."

"That was remarkably fast," said Gray, taken aback. "Clearly, for once, they weren't on strike."

"Seems not." Fowler, in his enthusiasm, missed the joke. Gray had to admit to himself it was a lame one anyway.

Hamson joined them, greeting Gray. She sat on the corner of the desk, one leg swinging. "Something to go on, at last," she said. "How did it go at the hospital?"

Gray updated them with brief details from the post mortem and his subsequent conversation with Natalie about Rachel's altercation with Khoury.

"He's still in town then," said Hamson.

"So it seems. Interesting that rather than running away from his pursuers, Khoury went after them with a knife."

"Yes."

Gray opened the file.

"Don't expect much," said Fowler. He and Hamson left Gray to it.

Gray started up his PC. There would be emails waiting, reports to file, the usual stuff. But his interest was in the French information. Even though Fowler had prepared him, Gray was disappointed by the scant data.

There was barely a page for each, comprising names, photos, country of origin. The other two appeared to be named Najjar and Shadid, all were from Syria. Najjar was the stabbing victim. An addendum stated that the French police believed there was a high probability that the names were false identities. And there were fingerprints for each of them.

There was no chance of obtaining records from their apparent homeland – Syria was more concerned with civil war and unrest than law and order. The only credible data was their temporary location in Calais (now out of date, of course) and the crimes they'd been accused of committing on French soil – robbery and indecent assault.

All had been residents in the area on the edge of Calais called the Jungle. A mix of temporary and semi-permanent accommodation where refugees, mainly men, sheltered while trying to cross into Britain – whose welfare system, the apparent wealth of employment, and its liberal attitude made it a magnet for migrants.

The Jungle had been a constant source of tension between the UK and France and was rarely out of the news. The Calais residents hated it too. Travel through the area to the ports became harder and harder. Night time was particularly hazardous with trucks and cars regularly stopped and boarded. About a year ago, the French finally had enough and shut the Jungle down and dispersed the refugees. It wasn't clear where they were supposed to have been sent.

At the back of the report was a final page stating the details for a contact in the Calais police, Inspector Jacques Morel. Sounded like a mushroom to Gray. He thought about what Carslake had told him yesterday. Tom had been seen on the way through Dover to Calais. Maybe Morel could help here as well?

Two birds, one stone. Gray picked up the phone and tapped in the numbers. Someone had even helpfully provided the international dialling code. The connection was made and the single tone vibrated in Gray's ear.

"*Oui?*" A woman's voice. Then an intelligible rattle of vowels and consonants Gray was unable to decipher.

Gray asked for Morel, adding a *s'il vous plaît* at the end.

The woman switched to accented English. "Who is calling?"

"Sergeant Gray, with Kent Police in the UK." The two police forces spoke a lot, particularly the coastal divisions.

"He is not here right now."

"When will he be back?"

"Sorry, I do not know. Would you like to leave a message?"

Gray sighed, left his details, said *au revoir* and, frustrated, ended the call.

"Unable to reach Morel?" said Fowler.

"Yes."

"Join the club. Neither could I or Yvonne."

Gray had an idea. The witness to Tom's disappearance was a few miles outside the Dover ferry port. Carslake had said he'd arrange for Gray to see them so he could combine that with a trip to France.

A couple of minutes on his desktop showed him the Calais police station was in the town centre and that there were plenty of tickets available on the Dover ferry. The sooner he went, the sooner he could be in Dover.

He entered his credit card details. A mouse click confirmed he'd bought a ticket which would be sent to him electronically.

Minutes later, he found Hamson at the murder board in the incident room. The section had been updated to include Khoury's name and details.

"I called Morel," said Gray. "I couldn't reach him."

"Surprise, surprise."

"I think I should go over there, see the inspector for myself."

"You've got be joking, Sol. No free holiday for you."

"We need to know what we're dealing with. The dossier gives us nothing other than a name."

Hamson paused, thinking about it. "I don't disagree, but we're short on manpower right now, and I'm not convinced you'll learn much more anyway. Everything French police had was on those pages. So, it's a no. I need you here, helping with the case."

"There's other stuff going on, Von." Gray could feel his anger growing. He was fighting to keep his voice even.

"Ma'am or boss please, Sergeant. And it's still a no."

"I'll talk to Carslake if I have to."

"Go ahead. I doubt he'll be any more willing than me."

"Okay."

"Seriously?" Hamson appeared ready to say something else but gritted her teeth instead. Gray left the incident room, Hamson trailing just behind. He went upstairs, walked straight past Sylvia, knocked on Carslake's door, and entered without waiting. The room was dominated by a large window overlooking the North Sea. Carslake was seated at his desk, silhouetted by the back lighting. He was talking on his mobile. He frowned at the intrusion. Gray stood before his desk, Hamson beside him, her arms crossed. Carslake ended the call and put his mobile down.

"Bloody wait for me to say you can come in next time, Sol," said Carslake.

"I want to go to Calais to see the French police about Khoury, the missing man."

"I know who he is. DI Hamson has been keeping me up to date. Why?"

"The information we have from them is useless. I'm sure knowing more will help us track him down."

Hamson stepped in. "Sir, this is a waste of time. I've already refused DS Gray's request because the loss in time travelling to and from France versus the potential benefit is minimal. Having his focus here is the best use for him."

"Sounds perfectly reasonable to me. So why are we having this conversation?"

"Because DI Hamson said I could take it up with you," said Gray. "And here I am, taking it up with you."

Carslake sighed. He waved for Gray and Hamson to be seated. "Go on, Sol. Tell me why I should override a senior officer's order."

"Because she's wrong." Hamson sucked in a breath. Gray could feel her anger, but he ignored her; there were bigger issues at stake. Tom issues. "Tom went through Calais, and I want to meet the witness."

"Ten years ago, Sol. The trail is cold."

"I have to try, Jeff. You told me I could meet the witness." Frustration was now creeping in. Why wouldn't either of them understand?

"What's going on?" asked Hamson.

"Somebody saw Tom being taken on a ferry to France."

Carslake stood up and stared out the window. Gray struggled to keep quiet, to let Carslake consider.

Eventually Carslake said, "It's a no to France."

"I've already booked a ticket on the first ferry crossing tomorrow morning!"

"Then you'll have to get a refund!" Carslake sat down. "Look, I know you're disappointed but Yvonne is correct. You're best used here."

"This is bullshit, Jeff!"

"You forget who you're talking to, DS Gray."

The atmosphere was brittle. Gray realised he'd gone too far, though he wouldn't be apologising. "What about the witness?" he said. "I have to see him."

"I've already said I'll arrange it. Now get out of here, both of you."

Dismissed, Gray left the office, Hamson on his heels. She stopped him at the top of the stairs.

"I fully appreciate how important Tom is to you. But why don't you try working with me rather than attempting to steamroller your way through whatever obstacle's in front?"

"Yes ma'am."

Hamson stared at Gray for a few moments before she spun on her heel and headed back to Carslake's office.

Gray would be going to France, and he would be seeing the witness.

Twenty Two

Gray went to the detective's office to collect his coat. He expected Hamson and Carslake would talk, then she would find Gray and attempt to justify herself all over again. He couldn't be bothered with it.

The Lighthouse Project was little more than half a mile away and there was no point in driving. Gray turned up his collar and got walking. There was a choice of routes – sea shore or residential. He decided on urban, so he turned right out of the station up the incline of Fort Road.

A few hundred yards along was the faded relic of the Winter Gardens, a popular entertainment venue of decades past, cut into the soft chalk cliff. Opposite, he turned into the narrow thoroughfare of Trinity Square.

The junction was overlooked by what had once been four-storey family houses for the middle class with superb sea views, but were now divided up into flats for people who probably never saw each other. It wouldn't have surprised Gray if Jake owned most of them. Off the main drag were less grandiose terraced houses but they too hadn't escaped being turned into multi-residence properties. The population density around here had dramatically increased over recent years.

Trinity Square itself was no longer. Maybe at one time it had been a pleasant space of green. Now it was the revenue-generating, ash-coloured, concrete-and-white lines of a car park. Here, another idea occurred to Gray. It would mean some subterfuge and he wouldn't be able to see the witness, but at least he could make it to France unhindered by Hamson and Carslake.

He pulled out his mobile and made a call while he carried on by corner shops, a pub, and the lawyers who'd handled both his dead wife's last will and testament and his recent property trades. All things to all people, living and deceased. By the time he reached the law courts, Gray was connected to an operator at the ferry company he'd originally booked with. He cancelled his ticket.

As he progressed along the border of the New Town, Gray called Eurostar. He could get a ticket on the first train out. It meant an extremely early start and a much higher price than the ferry, but the journey time was only thirty minutes. He could be back much faster. As he turned into Belgrave Road, he received confirmation of the reservation. He thanked the operator and ended the call.

The Lighthouse Project was just beyond the point where the two lanes of traffic split to pass either side of a row of houses. Gray paused. Above the entrance to the shelter was a small, hand-painted sign, black on a white background, a crude depiction of a lighthouse, probably the one at North Foreland on the edge of Margate, the last in the country to be operated by a human keeper. All were monitored via computer now, the cottages in the grounds given over to holidaymakers.

A handful of steps led to the wood-panelled front door, which was closed, bay windows either side of the entrance, sash picture windows on the next floor which needed a lick of paint or three. Net curtains blocked the view inside. Gray trotted up the crumbling sandstone steps, avoided the rusting railing. There was clearly no money in charity.

He rang the bell. It made no sound. Either the batteries were dead or the chime was out the back. It was a pity places like the outreach centre had to exist. A poor indictment of society. His second, louder thump was answered by a tall, young, skinny man.

"We're closed right now," he said.

Gray showed his warrant card. "I'm looking for Kelvin."

"Why?"

"I understand there was an altercation here last night. I interviewed Miss Peace earlier."

"Oh. That's me. You'd better come in." He opened the door wide, allowing Gray to step into a grubby hallway with several doors off it. There was an odour of man inside which Kelvin seemed used to. Unclean man. Body odour, unwashed clothes. Stale food.

Kelvin led Gray through the hall and into a back room; a refectory, judging by the benches and tables. There was a bedroom area off to one side. The smell was stronger here. Gray switched to breathing through his mouth. Kelvin, oblivious to the stench, headed into a small kitchen separated from the public area by a farm-style door, the ones which split in the middle, denying entry while allowing interaction.

Kelvin held up a jar of instant coffee. Gray declined. Kelvin made himself one, using hot water from a stainless steel urn and milk from a bottle he sniffed first. Kelvin pointed Gray to a seat at the first of the tables back in the refectory.

"I never asked what your surname is," said Gray.

"Askew. My mum always said it was a good name for a detective."

"Okay."

"Do you get it? Ask you?"

"Very good, Kelvin. Tell your mother it's funny."

Kelvin's face fell. "I can't. She died last year."

Gray felt pressure behind his eyes, like someone was gently pushing with their thumbs. He recognised it as sadness. Sadness for a woman he'd never met. "My condolences, Kelvin."

"You weren't to know." Kelvin forced a smile. "What can I do for you?"

"When I interviewed Natalie she said you let two men through."

Kelvin's face collapsed. "I wish I never had."

"Natalie intimated they paid you. Is that correct?"

"God, no! Why would she say that? I was just scared. I should have stood up to them like Rachel did. Maybe now it would be me lying in a hospital bed. I bet that's what Natalie would prefer."

"You don't like Natalie?"

"She's decent enough."

When Kelvin offered no more, Gray decided to change tack briefly, see if he could come at this in a direction more palatable to Kelvin. "Why do people volunteer?" he asked.

"Depends." Kelvin shrugged. "Different reasons."

"What about you?"

"At first, it was to get out of the house. It's difficult getting a job round here. Really, I just wanted to help people who can't always help themselves."

"How long has Rachel worked at the Lighthouse?"

"Nearly a year, long enough to know she'll stay. Most people come in for a short stint, struggle with the late nights, the sometimes-difficult subjects, and throw the towel in. Not Rachel. She's determined."

"What about Natalie?"

"Haven't a clue, probably forever. She never speaks about herself. You know she lives in the flat above?"

"No."

"Well she does. So she's here all the time, keeping an eye on things, talking to our guests, making sure the staff are okay, ranting at the council to get more funding. She never stops, but it's always about others. Natalie's very caring. But if we go out for a drink she refuses the invite every time."

"Sounds like a saint." Another shrug from Kelvin. "What about the man they were looking for. Do you remember him?"

"It was the one in the newspaper; the guy you're looking for."

"Are you sure?"

Kelvin nodded. "The two men, they had a photo."

"What do you mean?"

"A photo they were comparing our guests with. I found it screwed up on the floor."

"Where is it now?"

Kelvin pulled a piece of paper out from a pocket. "I thought you might want it."

Gray took it. The print was wrinkled and creased where it had been folded and screwed up. Gray was taken aback. The print was of Khoury from the CCTV Fowler had grabbed. Where had they got this from? It wasn't an image the police had released to the press.

"Did you recognise either of them?" asked Gray.

Kelvin didn't immediately answer, chewing his lip instead. Gray let him think. "It's why I stepped back."

"Who was it, Kelvin?"

"He's called Larry."

"Muscles, shaven head?" asked Gray. "Larry Lost?"

"That's him."

Gray could understand why Kelvin had been intimidated. Larry Lost was known locally as "Loser". A down-at-heel crook who worked on the door of equally down-at-heel establishments. He was too risky for nightclubs, when there was usually a heady mix of the small hours and large amounts of alcohol. After a series of insalubrious incidents, none of them would touch him. He was bad for business.

So that just left pubs and, of those, only the arse-end places where it didn't matter if someone with limited self-control started swinging as long as the fight was over and the trouble dispersed before the cops turned up. If they bothered at all.

Loser was Frank McGavin's man. McGavin was the local crime boss who ran everything illegal in Thanet, although the police had been unable to make any accusation against him stick.

"What about the other one?"

"I didn't recognise him."

"What did he look like?"

"Black guy, dreadlocks and a beard."

"Would you mind coming down to the station and looking over some photos?"

"Do I have to?"

Twenty Three

Back at the station, Gray showed Kelvin several photographs. The third was Larry Lost.

"That's him," said Kelvin.

"Are you sure?"

Kelvin nodded. Gray kept showing Kelvin photos but none appeared to be Larry's accomplice.

"Sorry," said Kelvin eventually.

"That's okay. You've been very helpful anyway. If you can wait here I'll get someone to take a statement."

"Then can I go? Natalie asked me to keep an eye on the Lighthouse while she's out."

"We'll get through it as fast as possible."

"I hope so."

Gray found a uniform to take care of Kelvin before he went looking for Hamson to bring her up to date. In the incident room, Hamson was standing before the murder board, the team ready for a briefing.

"Perfect timing, Sol. Mike has gathered some valuable information everyone needs to be aware of." Hamson nodded at Fowler. He stepped forward. Gray leaned against the wall at the back of the room.

"I've managed to piece together Regan Armitage's final movements. First, I reviewed the council-maintained cameras to plot his general direction that evening, working backwards from Seagram's. Once I'd figured out his route, uniform followed up with visits to establishments with CCTV to collect any additional footage. And we got this."

Fowler bent down, clicked a mouse and an overhead shot from a camera played on the large television screen. The video was a collection of clips meshed together, each time-stamped and organised consecutively, displaying Regan moving around Margate, from pub to bar to pub, the night he disappeared. The footage was grainy and indistinct at times, much sharper in others, some in monochrome, or in colour depending on the quality of the equipment.

"Initially," said Fowler, "there's not a great deal to interest us. Regan was by himself for most of the evening. He says hello to some people, shares a joke, but when transiting between pubs it's a solo affair." Fowler jumped forward through the video to illustrate his point. "Each place he visits, Regan stands eyeing the crowd. Usually for a few minutes; never more than a quarter of an hour."

"He's looking for somebody?" said Gray.

"Maybe, but who? It's when Regan gets to Seagram's that it becomes more intriguing."

Fowler let the scene play itself out. The time stamp read 22.32. An external shot from some distance, and at least one floor up; Regan skirting the long queue and going straight in. The view switched to the interior; Regan walking past the ticket booth. Then in black and white along a dimly lit corridor towards the camera; the perspective distorted at the edges by the fisheye lens before the view switched to him moving away and towards bright, strobing lights.

The time display jumped forward to 23.39. In reverse, Regan heading towards the camera, the nightclub lights at his back. He wasn't alone. The lens flared repeatedly as the strobing lights from the dance floor spilled out, making it difficult to distinguish his companion. When the viewpoint shifted to the nightclub entrance hall, Regan's partner was clearly a woman in a revealing dress and hair cut into a shoulder-length bob.

External once more; Regan staggering as he exited. The woman steadied Regan, helped him stay upright. One of the bouncers glanced at the pair, but returned his attention to the queue.

Fowler paused the playback. "That's the last we can find of Regan on any camera. He just disappears. No one sees him again until he washes up on the beach, hours later, dead."

"Thanks, Mike," said Hamson. "The key question is, 'who's the woman?' She might be the last person to see him alive. Sol, can you go down to Seagram's with Mike and interview the staff. We need an identification, if possible."

"We'll go this evening," said Gray.

"Okay."

"Drinks on the house, hopefully," said Fowler.

"I've got some other information," said Gray. "Turns out Khoury stayed the night at a local refuge, the Lighthouse Project on Belmont Avenue. And there were two men trying to find him during the early hours. They had this." Gray held out the photo of Khoury. "It's our photo, not the one we released to the press."

"Who the hell gave them that?"

There was silence in the room.

"One of the men was Larry Lost," said Gray.

"Loser? You're sure?"

"I've just had the witness pick out his mug shot." Gray checked his watch. "Right now, Loser will either be in bed or working." There was always a pub open somewhere in Thanet, if you fancied getting hammered.

"Find him."

Twenty Four

Khoury had spent half the day watching the Lighthouse Project, waiting for her return. Earlier, he'd walked the area, getting to know the backstreets and alleys; potential escape routes should he need them. He noticed quite a few people hanging around with seemingly little to do, standing on street corners, leaning against lamp posts, sitting on the steps of houses watching the world go by.

Nobody paid them any attention and vice versa. Khoury soon understood why. A number of facilities similar to the Lighthouse Project, with signs above the door, peppered the area. Despite this, he felt exposed and took to walking a little, pausing a little, following a circuitous route.

Last night, Khoury had left the Lighthouse at a run, keen to put distance between himself and the police, all the while keeping an eye out for Larry and his friend. He saw neither them nor the law. He grabbed a couple of hours' sleep in a shop doorway, until he was woken, stiff and freezing, by a passing bin lorry. He was still cold and getting hungry.

He halted a hundred yards away from the Lighthouse and sat on a wall. As his backside was growing sore, the front door opened. Two men stepped outside. One he recognised as Kelvin, the other, a tall, grey-haired man he hadn't seen before. He moved like police. They walked down the steps and turned towards the seafront. Khoury considered following them, but it was Natalie he needed to see. A few minutes later, he walked up the steps to the Lighthouse and knocked. No one answered. He went back to his route.

As the middle of the day approached, an old yellow VW Golf trundled by the Lighthouse and parked a hundred yards or so along. Natalie was behind the wheel. She looked tired and haggard. Khoury pushed off the metal fence opposite the Lighthouse and made his way over. Natalie didn't notice him. She climbed the steps, fished around in her bag for her keys, and selected one from a decent-sized bunch.

While Natalie was turning the key, Khoury went up the steps. She glanced over her shoulder when his shadow fell. The door was already open a crack. Khoury pushed it wide and bundled Natalie through. She stumbled into the hall, tripping on the carpet, and fell onto her knees. The bag hit the floor and spilled its contents everywhere. Khoury kicked the door shut behind him.

Natalie rolled onto her backside, leaning away, hands on the floor, knees drawn up. Her expression changed with recognition. Fear crept into her face. Khoury looked down, feeling ashamed. This wasn't what he'd had in mind when he imagined a new life in the UK. But he had to do this. For Najjar. For Shadid. For the family he would never see again.

"What do you want?" she asked.

Khoury pulled Natalie to her feet and guided her forward through into the refectory, then the kitchen.

"Food," said Khoury.

Natalie blinked. She opened the fridge and pulled out a large, plastic tub. She put it on a work surface and peeled off the lid, the seal parting with a loud snap.

She spooned stew into a bowl, microwaved it for a couple of minutes, all the while keeping her eyes on him. His eyes darted nervously from the kitchen door, then back to Natalie. When the microwave pinged she took the bowl out and put the bowl on a table. Khoury indicated for her to slide onto one of the benches, then sat down to face her. He placed his knife on the table and ate quickly, glancing up at her with each slurp.

When he'd finished, he stood so he had the height advantage and dominance. He hated himself for frightening a woman. But if she thought he was dangerous, then she would cooperate. "Where is Larry?"

"Who?"

"Larry. He was here last night."

"Do you mean Larry Lost?"

"Yes. Where is he?"

"I don't know. He works in a couple of pubs. Why do you ask?"

"Write down the names."

"I'll need a pen and paper. They were in my bag, by the front door."

"Get it, then."

Natalie stood and went back into the hallway, Khoury right behind her in case she decided to make a dash. Natalie knelt down, swept fingers through her possessions on the floor, found what she wanted.

"Pass me your purse," said Khoury.

Natalie handed it over. Khoury opened the clasp and took out the few notes she had in there. He stuffed them into a pocket and dropped the purse on the floor.

Standing again, she rested the paper against the wall, wrote an address, and passed it to him. He glanced at the details, which meant nothing to him, before putting the paper into the same pocket as the cash. Khoury wasn't entirely satisfied, though. With Larry and Dave on his tail, and possibly the police, as well, he needed to minimise his movements, his exposure. "Anywhere else he might be?"

"I've told you all I know."

A thought occurred to him. "Does he have a boat?"

"I think so."

"Where?"

"Ramsgate, I would expect. It's the largest anchorage in the area."

Khoury remembered the words on the back of the boat when he'd thrown himself overboard. *Etna and Ramsgate*. A name and the port of registration. "I'm sorry, but I need your car." He held out his hand.

Natalie bent down, scooped up a key on a fob, and dropped it into Khoury's palm. He folded his fingers over it.

"You might warn your friend, Larry, that I'm coming for him."

"He's no friend of mine."

As Khoury considered his options, there was a knock at the door.

"That'll be Kelvin," said Natalie.

Another thump at the door and then the letterbox rattled. "Can you let me in?"

"Why don't I open up, and you just walk out of here?" Natalie asked Khoury. "There isn't a way out the back. It's the front or nowhere."

Khoury put his knife away, nodded at Natalie as the letterbox flapped once more. She took a couple of steps forward, undid the lock, opened the door wide, and stepped back against the wall to let Khoury pass. Kelvin was standing on the top step, looking bewildered and lost for words.

Khoury barged past him. Kelvin stumbled but didn't react. Natalie grabbed Kelvin by the wrist and dragged him inside. When Khoury looked over his shoulder, the door was slamming shut.

Khoury walked up the street until he reached Natalie's car. He got in, started the engine, and pulled straight out into traffic, ignoring the blare of a horn.

After a minute's drive Khoury reached some traffic lights. They were red. He slowed, looked at the signs. One pointed towards Ramsgate. There was the pictogram of a boat.

When the lights turned green, Khoury followed the arrow and kept doing so until the harbour spread out before him. A huge rectangle of calm water dotted with yachts and motor boats was protected by two harbour arms which didn't quite meet in the middle, leaving a small gap for the boats to head out the North Sea.

Khoury drove past a line of restaurants, looking for a space. He found one near a tall stone monument in the shape of a needle and a shiny silver burger van. He pulled in, switched off the engine, and looked at the various seagoing vessels. They were many, maybe even hundreds. Khoury didn't bother to lock the car. He took a slow trip around the circumference, trying to recognise Larry's craft.

He'd walked nearly all the way round by the time he spotted a possible candidate. He paused on a metal footbridge. The shape looked right. Long, low prow; and raked cabin, painted black. However, Khoury couldn't take a closer look as the jetty was barred by a metal gate and high fence to the side of which was a keypad. He tried the gate anyway, just in case. Firmly locked.

There were two ways to get in. Either drop off the harbour wall into the water where there was no fence, or climb over it. The former meant a twelve-foot plunge and a bit of a swim, so Khoury wasn't keen. He'd had enough of swimming. The latter meant awaiting darkness. Khoury decided on option two and returned to the stolen car.

Twenty Five

Gray pulled Larry's address from the Police National Computer – a bedsit in a tall terraced house in Cliftonville on Northdown Road, once one of the most salubrious areas in Thanet, but now one of the least.

Northdown Road, wide, busy, long, and possessing a rundown air, was the arterial route for traffic through Cliftonville. A line of shops ran along both sides of the street – charity places, takeaways, a bargain booze store, a cash converter, a pawn shop, a Polish supermarket, a few pubs, a Halal butcher's, a Caribbean fruit shop.

Getting inside the building had proved ridiculously straightforward. Gray simply pressed the buzzer of one of the many flats on a keypad beside the front door. It unlocked without him even making an excuse to the occupant he'd disturbed.

Fixed to the wall inside, creating a minor obstruction, was a black-painted metal box with individual flaps for the mail. Each had a lock, though all could be opened up by putting a finger into the gap at the top and tugging downwards. The majority had various takeaway menus sticking out. A quick way of reducing the pile to be delivered. Larry's was empty, even of junk mail. Gray moved past the box and closed the door behind him. The light level dropped dramatically. He flicked a nearby light switch. No change. The bulb overhead was dead.

The threadbare carpet was green and brown swirls. There were a couple of doors either side of the corridor, numbered one and two. Beneath the curve of the stairs were several bikes and a pushchair.

Floorboards creaked beneath Gray's feet as he headed upstairs, the same carpet design stretching upwards. A job lot laid decades ago. Larry's flat was in the eaves on the fourth floor, number eight. The landing was tiny with only a few feet of space with sufficient clearance above for him to stand upright. Gray thumped on the door. He listened for movement. Nothing. He knocked again. Still nothing.

He transferred his attention to number seven. The occupant opened up before Gray had even raised his fist. A man in his early twenties wearing matching black tracksuit top and bottoms, with a double white stripe on leg and sleeve. His hair was a shambles, bags under his eyes.

"You after Larry?" he said.

"Yes," replied Gray.

"Join the queue."

"Why's that?"

"Someone always is." The man shrugged.

"So why answer the door now?"

"It's obvious you're a copper, even through the peephole."

"Does Larry cause you any bother?"

"Not really. Looks scary, but get talking to him and it's pretty clear he's a mess. Is he in trouble?"

"I just want to speak to him in connection with an incident."

"What incident?"

"Confidential, sir."

"Like that, is it? I get it. He usually leaves a key under the carpet. Excuse me, would you?"

The man waved at Gray to move. The only way to create room was for Gray to drop down a couple of the steps. Once he had done so the neighbour bent over, peeled back a corner of the carpet. There, in the dust motes, was a key. The neighbour grinned at Gray like their numbers had come up in the lottery.

Gray closed the door on his newfound friend, who was craning to look inside so much he was in danger of falling flat on his face. Where Larry Lost was best described as large, the flat was the opposite.

About six feet out from the wall which met the landing, the roof descended at an angle. So everything which needed height was towards the right and vice versa. The kitchen was in the back corner. Opposite was a bed, and crammed in between was a single armchair and the television. The floor was polished boards with several rugs intermittently spaced.

The angular roof line turned back into vertical about three feet from the floor. Inset periodically were small hatches, Alice-in-Wonderland-like. Gray crossed to one of the cupboards. He bent down and popped the door open. A rug on the floor got in the way of its swing and he had to shift the carpet a few inches as a result.

Disappointingly there wasn't a portal to another place; no bottle marked "Drink Me", just clothes on hangers. He shut the door, resisted opening up again several times to see if the inside changed. It didn't.

A couple of Velux windows cut into the roof-provided light. One was open a crack. No danger of getting burgled this high up unless maybe by a seagull. The walls were bare except for the television and a photo of a boat.

As well as being small, the flat was surprisingly neat and tidy. Gray had expected a mess. Pigeon-holing Larry accordingly. He had been wrong.

The search took all of five minutes. Gray found a small bag of cannabis in the bedside cabinet. He looked out the window at the view over the adjacent roofs and towards the sea. He went back to the photo and looked at the boat. It was clearly moored in Ramsgate harbour. The Royal Yacht Club and the Smack Boys building behind were distinctive. Gray couldn't see a name. He took a photo with his camera.

He called Hamson. "Larry's not here."

"Found anything incriminating?"

"A bag of weed."

"Get yourself to Seagram's, Sol. Larry will turn up."

"I've got another lead I'm going to follow."

"Oh?"

"Larry owns a boat."

"I wouldn't have seen him as the seafaring type."

"Maybe he's the type who sails to France in the dead of night?"

Twenty Six

Gray drove inland, taking the dual carriageway past the defunct Kent International Airport rather than the less direct coastal route. It took just over twenty minutes to complete the journey. He went as far round Ramsgate harbour as he could, and parked by the footbridge. He was facing the Ramsgate Home for Smack Boys at the foot of Jacob's Ladder, a set of stairs which gave access from the clifftop high above, next to the Sailors' church, both built in the late 1800s. The smack boys were apprenticed to fishing boats and the building was where they stayed when not at sea.

He pulled out his phone and compared the angle at which he was currently standing with the photo on Larry's wall. He was too far over. He crossed the metal footbridge, which could be swung out of the way when ships needed access to the harbour, and checked the perspectives several times until it seemed about right. Then he focused on the boats in the immediate area. Eventually he saw one which was similar. But, a metal fence and a gate with a keypad blocked the jetties off from public access.

He tried the gate. Locked. He stared through the fence, but saw no one who he could ask to let him through. He turned around. Above him was a tower, glass around the circumference. The harbour master's office. His role was to keep a constant eye out for marine traffic and monitor it.

Gray walked over to the building. The lower floor was toilets and showers for those moored here. He found the office door and went inside, took the stairs. The view from the top was superb. Sea on one side, the bobbing ships on the other.

"Can I help you?" A bearded, bald-headed man who appeared to be in his fifties and wearing a naval uniform was frowning at the intrusion. He was holding a huge pair of binoculars he'd been using to scan the waterways. Gray pulled out his warrant card.

"I want to gain access to one of the boats moored here."

"Which one?"

"I don't know the name." Gray showed the harbour master the photo of Larry's boat.

"Ah, the Etna." The harbour master introduced himself as Captain Eadie.

"Do you know anything about the Etna's movements?"

"She comes and goes at all times of day and night. There's no routine to it."

"Do you know the owner?"

"Larry? I see him around."

"What's the code for the keypad?"

"1805. Battle of Trafalgar."

"Thanks, I'll only be a few minutes."

"I can keep a good eye on you with these." Eadie grinned and showed Gray the binoculars.

Gray made his way back outside again. At the keypad he tapped in the numbers. The magnetic lock powered off with a heavy clunk. Gray pushed on the gate, went through, and let it close behind him. The Etna was almost at the end of the jetty. Gray glanced around the exterior, not much to see.

He stepped aboard; momentarily caught out by the rocking motion he wasn't used to. Despite living by the sea for years he never spent any time on it. He tried the door which would give him access to the cabin. It was locked. The door was wood with some round glass panels at the top. He tapped the glass. It felt thin. Access would be easy. But if he did discover any evidence it would be inadmissible in court – no search warrant

He stepped off onto the jetty again and went back to his car. He always carried nitrile gloves in the boot. He grabbed a pair, along with a couple of evidence bags, and went back to the Etna. As he went back on board, he looked up at the harbour master's office. Eadie wasn't in sight. Gray didn't want to be caught.

Gray pulled on the gloves, drew his coat sleeve over his fist, and hit the glass with his knuckles a couple of times until it cracked. Once more and he had a break. He picked out the shards, reached through, and felt around. His fingertips brushed the knob of a Yale lock. Standing on his tiptoes, Gray was just able to get a grip. He twisted and the door popped open.

Inside was a cramped cabin, dimly lit as curtains covered the portholes. He put the glass shards down on a work surface. Using the torch on his phone, he first went through into the bedroom at the back. He returned to the galley kitchen. On the bottom shelf of a cupboard, which otherwise contained crockery, he found a tool box.

He lifted out the top drawer, which held a hammer and several screwdrivers. Beneath an oily rag were three ziplocked plastic bags of white powder. He picked one up. He opened the bag but couldn't identify the contents, and he wasn't keen to test some on himself. He poured some into an evidence bag, resealed the bag, and returned the rest of the powder to where he'd found it.

Before leaving, he moved the glass shards onto the floor, just inside the galley. Back on deck he shut the door behind him, peeled off the gloves, and made his way along the jetty.

When he was stepping through the gate, Eadie pulled back one of the windows in the tower and leaned out. "Find anything?" he shouted.

"Not this time."

"Better luck in the future."

When Gray was inside his car, he put the evidence bag beneath the passenger seat and checked his watch. He had time.

FINDING A PARKING SPOT outside the hospital was never easy so Gray put his car in the area reserved for the medical staff. His phone bleeped as he was applying the handbrake. It was Noble, suggesting a time to meet. Gray put him back by an hour as it overlapped with when he would be at Seagram's, interviewing the staff with Fowler.

Clough was in his cubbyhole office. Gray dropped the evidence bag onto the pathologist's desk. "Can you identify this?"

Clough eyed the bag before picking it up, seeking an explanation from Gray by his expression. When he didn't get one, Clough opened the bag, took a careful sniff. "Odourless. Wait here a minute." He left his office and was soon back with a small white cardboard box. He closed the door, put the box on the table, and pulled out a plastic cylinder about ten centimetres tall. He popped a cap off one end, withdrew an ampoule, opened this too before placing it upright on the desk.

He folded a piece of paper, scooped a little of the powder out of the evidence bag, and poured it into the ampoule. Inside the vial was a clear liquid; it began to darken as soon as the powder hit. He let the colour develop for half a minute before comparing the shade against a chart which he removed from the white cardboard box.

"Ketamine," he said.

"Are you certain?" asked Gray.

"Ninety-nine per cent. That's the accuracy of these kits."

"Thanks." Gray picked up the plastic bag, resealed it, and put it back into his pocket. He left Clough. There was another place he might be able to find Larry. Gray had some more questions to ask him now.

However, Larry would have to wait. Gray had to get to Seagram's; otherwise Hamson would crucify him.

Twenty Seven

Seagram's was on the edge of the Old Town, not far from the station and only a few minutes' walk from the Lighthouse Project.

The posters started a couple of streets away from the club. Gray hadn't really noticed them before. None of the offers appealed to him. Cheap drinks – double shots for one pound. Ladies nights – free entry for women but men had to pay. Over 30s nights and under 16s afternoons. With the pubs now able to open for extended hours they could behave as mini-nightspots themselves, which meant Seagram's was operating in a congested market.

When Gray reached the club the doors were shut: no bouncers, no queue. Also, no Fowler. Gray sent him a text asking where he was.

Gray rattled the doors. He stepped back, looked towards the CCTV. It was at the end of the building, large lenses mounted high for perspective and behind cages for protection. The cameras wouldn't miss much of anything.

His phone rang. Jake.

"We're closed."

"Even to me?" said Gray.

"Depends. Is this a social visit?"

"I was hoping to speak to your staff," said Gray. "About Regan."

"What about him?"

"He was here the night he disappeared. Someone might know something."

"Of course, no problem. Give me a moment to come down."

By the time Gray had returned the mobile to his pocket the door was swinging back on its hinges, Jake's face a white oval in the darkness. Gray stepped inside, Jake making way, shutting the door behind him.

There was the cash booth on one side, the corridor on the other. Along a few feet was the other CCTV camera. Gray looked up and down the area, recognising the perspective from Fowler's footage.

"You couldn't have picked a better time, actually," said Jake. "We're getting ready to open so most of my employees are in. Do you want to use my office?"

"Thanks. DS Fowler'll be here shortly."

"I remember him. I'll get someone to bring him up when he arrives."

Jake led Gray deeper into the club. The corridor opened up onto equally dim expansive dance floor. Illumination along the floor, some soft lighting in the ceiling, but little else. Jake strode forward. Gray hung back, his eyes firmly on where he was treading.

At the rear of the floor and through another set of doors Jake pointed to some stairs marked "Private, No Entry". Jake started the climb.

"Do you have any problem with drugs here?"

"Why do you ask?" Jake didn't turn around or pause.

"Nothing specific."

"Good, because I'd be all over anyone who dared to shift any product in my establishment."

"Glad to hear it."

FOWLER TURNED UP TEN minutes later and apologised for being late with no explanation offered as to why. Gray was seated on one of the two sofas in Jake's office that faced each other across a coffee table. Fowler placed himself on the same sofa and they agreed that Gray would ask questions while Fowler observed reactions and took notes.

The process began with the bouncers. Seagram's employed eight of them, but Gray was only interested in the pair who'd been working the front door the night Regan disappeared. They came in together. One was bulky in the way you'd expect a wrestler to be, the other was wiry and tough with quick eyes, the look of a boxer about him.

The wrestler was called Sam, the boxer Nigel.

"Yeah, we remember him, don't we, Sam?" Nigel's accent was West Country. Sam nodded, eyes roving the room.

"Arriving or leaving?" asked Gray.

"Both. He went in on his own, left with a woman."

"Could you describe her?"

"Blue hair," said Sam. He was a local. Nigel nodded.

"Anything else about her?" asked Gray.

The bouncers looked at each other, back at Gray. They shrugged.

"Height, weight, build, what she was wearing?"

"Not really," said Nigel. "Just remember the hair."

"Yep," said Sam. "It was blue."

"Did you see her entering the club?"

"No," said Nigel after a few moments' thought. "But we were busy. And there'd been some bother to sort out."

"But you recall her leaving?"

"'Cos she was with Mr Armitage. There's always somebody with him."

"What do you mean?"

"Liked the girls. It was a mission."

"Yeah, conquests," said Sam.

"You admired that trait in Regan?"

"Who wouldn't say no to a free bit of skirt?" said Nigel. "Perk of the job, right?"

"Is it?"

Nigel shrugged.

"Did Regan have any enemies?" asked Gray.

Nigel and Sam looked at each other again, then back to Gray in what seemed to be a habitual cross reference. "No," said Nigel.

"No friends neither," said Sam.

Gray didn't get anything else meaningful from the bouncers and let them go after a few more questions. It was the same with the young woman who'd been on the ticket booth; she'd been too busy dealing with guests to notice Regan at all.

"He's part of the furniture," she'd said, pulling a face but not elaborating why.

Next Gray spoke to the front of house and bar staff. None had engaged with Regan directly that night. To a person, they were complimentary, said he was a nice guy, always had a word for them, no freebies, paid for everything, expected nothing, and tipped well. To all intents and purposes Regan seemed to be the perfect customer.

Gray got a return for his efforts on interview number six. A tattooed guy, more ink than skin, settled into the seat opposite. Tunnel earrings which stretched the lobes into large hollows, short, spiky hair shaved to the skull at the sides. He wore a t-shirt to best show the markings off – colour up the arms and on his neck. The fabric concealed plenty of muscle too. He looked like he could handle himself.

"Ray Quigley," he said when Gray enquired. "Bar manager. Used to be on the doors, worked myself up to senior management." He puffed his chest out.

"Did you see Regan on Saturday night?"

"Yes and I served him, like I always do."

"Always?"

Quigley nodded though didn't elaborate.

"What time was this?"

Quigley shrugged. "Hard to say."

"Make a guess."

"Early, we'd only just got really going. Time flies, we get very busy. It's all I can do to keep up with the punters. Before you know it, midnight has been and gone and we're closing up. I get maybe fifteen minutes off for a smoke."

"When?"

"Eleven if I'm lucky, as long as I'm not dealing with any problems."

"Such as?"

"Stupid staff, usually. Short-changing the customers, particularly the pissed ones. They think no one'll notice. Quick way to make a bit of extra cash."

"Did you see Regan before or after your smoke break?"

A sigh from Quigley, though he paused. His eyes glanced up and left as he accessed his memory. "Before."

"So what time?"

"Ten? Ten thirty?"

"That's as specific as you can be?"

"Afraid so."

"Do you know all your customers?"

"A lot of them. Margate's a small town; we're the best night spot. Clean as a whistle, virtually no trouble, plenty of fun. We get regulars, regularly. And he's the boss's son."

"Did you see Regan with anyone?"

"He was alone when he came to the bar."

"What was he drinking?"

"Estrella Reserva. We bring it in just for him."

"You don't sell it to anyone else?"

"We're not allowed to."

"Who tells you not to?"

"Him. Regan. We ran out once. He was..." Quigley clamped his jaw. It was clear to Gray the bar manager knew he'd said too much.

"He was what?"

"Fine," mumbled Quigley. "No problem at all."

"Angry? Apoplectic?"

"No."

It was pretty obvious what Quigley really thought. "You didn't like Regan much, then?"

"He's the boss's son."

The phrase was like a mantra. "Does that mean you can't have an opinion?"

"It means, he's the boss's son."

"What about Cameron?"

"He's the boss's son too?" Quigley opened him arms in a question mark, rolled his eyes.

Gray got more specific. "Do you ever see him here?"

"Cameron? Once or twice. Clubs don't really seem to be his sort of thing."

"You said Seagram's is clean."

"Yes." Quigley frowned. "As a whistle." The same phrase that Jake had used.

"You've never seen any drugs here?"

Quigley stared straight at Gray. "No. Look, I've got to get back to work."

Gray raised an eyebrow at Fowler to see if he had any questions. Fowler shook his head. Gray let Quigley go, and he didn't hang about.

"He's got more to say," said Gray.

"Definitely," agreed Fowler, "but not here and not now."

The thump of music was coming up the stairs, clear through the door which Quigley had left standing open.

"How much CCTV footage did you get?"

"From here? All of it. From opening to closing."

"Did you see the blue-haired woman going in?"

Fowler thought about it. "I don't think so."

"Okay, we'll need to look again. Blue hair, it might be a wig."

"A disguise?"

"It would make her stand out, that's for sure. We need to find her. See who sells wigs locally, maybe they'll remember somebody buying a blue one." Fowler recorded the action in his notebook. "And we can make an educated guess at what Regan was up to before he arrived at the club."

"Trawling for women," agreed Fowler.

There was a knock at the door, Jake was leaning in. He said, "Feels strange, asking permission to come into my own office."

Gray wondered how much Jake had overheard.

"Do you want to see anyone else? We're open, and we'll be getting busy soon."

Gray glanced at his watch. It had been an hour. "We're done for now, I think."

"Want a drink before you go? If you're off-duty, of course."

"Sounds good to me," said Fowler.

"I'll pass. Got an early start tomorrow." Gray was feeling unwell again, a pressure and burning behind his breastbone.

"Your loss," said Jake. He led them downstairs and across the dance floor. It was lit now, as was the bar. Quigley was behind the counter, restocking.

Jake got Quigley's attention. "Give Sergeant Fowler whatever he wants," he said before shaking both their hands and leaving.

"I'll have a beer," said Fowler.

"We've got some Estrella Reserva going spare," said Quigley.

"That'll do me fine."

"Do you have CCTV behind the bar, Ray?" asked Gray.

Quigley pointed to a tiny camera mounted on the wall above the tills. "That's how I know if the staff is fiddling."

"Nowhere else?"

"No." There wouldn't be a view of the bar or dance floor from the lens.

"Are you sure you won't stay?" asked Fowler.

"I've got to go."

Fowler raised the bottle in a salute. Gray left him to it. He had a date in The English Flag.

Twenty Eight

Then

It was very early in the morning when Regan Armitage reached his home. Inside he could clearly hear his father talking to someone; maybe shouting was more accurate. Regan had hoped to creep in unnoticed and slip into bed while everyone was asleep. His foot was on the bottom step of the stairs when he caught the words "fire" and "deaths". A shudder ran through him.

He opened the door to his father's office. A lamp spilled out a circle of light. His father, in dressing gown and pyjamas, was standing behind his desk, head down, revealing a developing bald patch, talking on his phone. His free hand was curled into a fist, the knuckles pressing into the wood.

"Okay, see that you do," said Jake. "This is going to cause a whole load of shit for me." He finished the call, dropped the mobile onto the desk. Regan stared at his father until the older man realised he wasn't alone. He glanced at Regan before his eyes returned to the telephone.

"What the hell are you doing?" Jake asked; no strength in his words. "You should be in bed." He sagged into a chair. His face was drawn and pale.

"It was me," Regan said.

Jake leant over and grabbed a glass and a bottle. He poured himself a drink, took a mouthful, and swallowed. "What was?"

"The fire. I did it."

"This is no joke, son."

"I'm telling the truth." Regan shrugged the backpack off and unzipped it. He pulled out the petrol can and held it towards his father.

Jake slowly put the glass down and rose, as if seeing Regan clearly now. Jake walked over, took the can, sniffed it. A little petrol sloshed around in the bottom. Jake dropped the can and grabbed Regan by the shoulders, his fingers digging in. "Tell me everything," he said.

"I heard you saying you wanted rid of the old bat so you could start work on a new project. I thought I'd help things along."

"By setting fire to her house?"

Regan nodded. "It was the best I could do."

"Oh my God." Jake let go of Regan, turned away, and tugged at his hair as if he were going to rip it out. He swung back to Regan. "Do you know what you've done? There were people still inside the building!"

"I tried to ring the fire brigade, but the phone was broken."

"A family burned to death!"

"Nobody saw me."

"If this comes out, I'll be ruined. You'll end up in prison, Regan!"

"I've got away with it."

"Not yet, you haven't. There'll be an investigation." Jake returned to his desk, poured himself another drink, and swallowed it in one. "Are you sure you weren't seen?"

Regan nodded. "There was a girl, but I stayed in the shadows until she'd gone."

"Okay, maybe this can be dealt with." Jake picked up his mobile again and made a call.

JAKE WAS STILL DRINKING when Jeff Carslake arrived. Regan could smell the smoke from the fire on Carslake's clothes. He shuddered again. With the office door closed, Carslake asked Regan to repeat his story, word for word.

When Regan was done, Carslake said, "Yes, we can fix this." Carslake took the backpack, said he'd dispose of it. "One of the firemen at the scene said he suspected it was arson. There's no chance of hiding that aspect."

"What are you suggesting then?" asked Jake.

"I'll probably just fit someone else up for it. There's a couple of fire starters that I could point the finger at, though an accident would be better."

"Whatever it takes, whatever it costs to keep Regan out of jail, just do it."

Twenty Nine

N^{ow} The English Flag was a pub in Margate's Old Town. To call the establishment down-at-heel would be a kindness. It was down-at-sticky-carpet. The pub was resisting the area's gentrification with a two-finger salute to the London set and immigrants in equal measure. As the immediate area grew more respectable, so the Flag seemed to dip further.

Inside, a huge George Cross flag hung behind the bar, held up by nails at each corner. Otherwise it was tacky floors, worn furniture, and an appalling attitude to customer service. It served beer, a limited range of spirits, and monkey nuts, delivered with derision by the surly landlord, all day. This was where the dregs of Margate came to drown their sorrows.

However, there was a camaraderie between the clientele. A one-for-all attitude. Certainly not friendship but a kinship at least. Newcomers were viewed with suspicion until they were trusted. The regulars knew exactly who Gray was and, like a cat about to strike, shrank into themselves. Gray, though, wasn't here for a fight. He was here for answers.

Noble was seated at the bar, leaning on the stained wood as if supporting himself. Within the crook of his forearms stood a pint. A bandage was wound around his head, tufts of hair poking out.

"You got out quickly," said Gray. He sat down. He still wasn't feeling great; the fresh air hadn't done anything to relieve his feeling of wanting to be sick.

"I discharged myself," said Noble. "Bloody doctors. They haven't a clue."

"Brain surgery, was it?"

Noble ignored Gray's flippancy. "Want one?"

"From here? You've got to be joking."

Noble shrugged and sank a good portion of his pint. "When you've had a near-death experience like I have, best to make every moment count."

"It's lucky you possess such a thick skull, Will."

"Very funny." Noble turned, held out a hand to Gray. "Thanks for looking out for me, though."

"It's my job." Gray shook Noble's hand. "And I'm sure you'd do the same."

Noble betrayed a doubtful look.

"What happened?" asked Gray.

"Not here." Noble jinked his thumb, indicating a table as far from the bar as possible. "Walls have ears." The landlord was standing nearby, slowly splitting monkey nuts and chewing on the contents and taking in everything. He was known to sell anything for cash.

When they were seated Noble said, "Speaking of which, all of this stays between us, right?"

"That depends on what you tell me."

"I've always liked you, Sol. But the company you keep, it bothers me."

"What do you mean?"

"Carslake's not a straight shooter."

"What makes you say that?" Gray

Noble shook his head. "I don't trust him and neither should you."

"Why not? I've known Jeff for years."

"That's your problem." Noble stared at Gray for a long moment. "Some stuff I've heard over the years. I think he has some associations a cop just shouldn't have. Like with Regan Armitage."

"Do you have any proof?"

"Beyond seeing them at social events together over the years? No, just whispers from contacts. Carslake's clever."

"If you're going to throw accusations like that around you'd better be sure you have the evidence, Will."

"We're just talking, Sol."

Gray let it pass. "What happened at your offices yesterday?"

"I was minding my own business when two men came in. They said I had something they wanted."

"What?"

"That was just the problem, they didn't say at first. You know how I am, kindly soul and all that, I'll do anything for anyone." Gray managed to keep his face restrained. It wasn't more than a minute since Noble had failed to commit to helping Gray. "When I said I hadn't a clue what they wanted they locked me in the cupboard and began turning the place over. I'm thinking they're going to kill me. Anyway, after they'd busted the place up good and proper they let me out into fresh air. I nearly died in there, I tell you."

"Poisoned by your own atmosphere?"

"Now you're just being rude."

"And?" prompted Gray.

"I couldn't believe my eyes. It was like a hurricane had torn through the office, turned everything upside down. Bastards. I told them so too. They asked me again if I had it. And when I said, again, that I had no idea what they were talking about, this time they told me. Millstone."

"Millstone?"

Noble nodded. "The property developers. We talked about them the other day."

"We did?"

"Jesus, Sol! Outside the Lighthouse. They're the ones trying to tear the town down."

Gray remembered now. He had the protest leaflet still in his desk drawer at the station. "Oh, yeah."

"I had a bit of a search around the office, pretending to look and that was when it all went a bit pear-shaped."

"Why?"

"Because I went for them. Managed to get a couple of knuckles on a chin. I was doing all right until his mate hit me. I went down like a sack of spuds, Sol." Noble put a hand to the back of his head, touched the bandage gently. "One made a call while I was on the floor. Told someone they couldn't find it and asked if they should finish me off. I nearly shit myself. I thought, this is the end of me. The person on the other end must have said no cause they left, and I got in touch with you." Noble eyed Gray balefully. "Eventually."

"Who did they call?"

"No names were used."

"Tell me about Millstone."

"Not much to say really," said Noble with a shrug, "as there's not much to find. Believe me, I've tried. They're newly formed, no apparent trading history, no accounts yet. The company address is in Jersey. Offshore, invisible. All this talk of increasing transparency." Noble shook his head. "Really, it's a sham. Big businesses paying little to no tax. Evasion versus avoidance? They're one and the same as far as I'm concerned. We should all pay what we can, Sol."

"No argument from me."

"One thing I do know, Millstone have got Jake Armitage in their sights. They want him out. Margate's becoming big business, and it seems Millstone, whoever they are, are after a major share of it."

"Did you recognise who attacked you?"

Noble nodded. "Larry Lost and some guy with dreadlocks."

"They keep turning up."

"Frank McGavin wants in on the act as well. He's moved into property. The new fish restaurant on the Broadstairs seafront? It's McGavin's."

Gray raised an eyebrow, McGavin was changing his tactics. Property and restaurants. Very upmarket.

"Jake is being squeezed, Sol. Between Millstone and McGavin. I'd bet it's not a pleasant place to find yourself."

"Is this the story you said you were working on? The big one?"

"I'm saying nothing." Noble grabbed hold of Gray's forearm. "I owe you one."

"Think of me as your guardian angel, Will."

"There was one other thing which stuck in my mind. When they were on the phone Larry mentioned Sunset."

"What does that mean, Will?"

"I think he was referring to the guest house fire."

"I don't understand."

"Me neither. I thought I'd mention it. Just watch yourself with all this, all right? Remember what I said about Carslake. It's for you only." Gray wondered what Noble meant about Carslake and the part all this played in an increasingly complex puzzle.

"I'd better be going, Will. Thanks for the information." Gray stood up. He felt dizzy. Outside, the pub door swinging shut behind him, Gray's stomach began to lurch. He ran for the rear of the pub, a car park, and threw up against the wall, heaving until there was no more.

Gray stood, bent at the waist, hands on thighs, trying to get his breath back. He hoped he'd be well enough to catch the train tomorrow morning. At least when he rang Hamson to complain of an illness he wouldn't be lying.

Thirty

Khoury jolted awake when the car door closed. He sat up; blinked the sleep out of his eyes. It was dark outside. A streetlight nearby cast a weak yellow hue which barely illuminated the pavement beneath.

There was a man sitting in the passenger seat next to him. A big man, wearing a sharp suit. His head was shaven to the skin. Which puzzled Khoury as he'd locked the doors before he drifted off. The man grinned at him, though there was no humour, just brilliant-white teeth. Through the windscreen Khoury saw a second man, with familiar dreadlocks, sitting on a bollard staring directly at him. He was one of the men who'd been searching for him at the Lighthouse. Dave.

"I hear you've been trying to find an associate of mine," said the man in the passenger seat, staring straight ahead, not bothering to look in Khoury's direction. Khoury wondered if he could get to his knife quickly. The man's hands rested on his thighs. He wore gloves. The sight of them turned Khoury's guts to ice. No fingerprints. "You're looking for Larry? Is that right?"

Khoury nodded.

"I'm Frank, by the way," he finally turned to face Khoury. "Frank McGavin."

Khoury saw no one else outside besides Dave. The harbour master's office, which had a seagull's-eye view of the immediate area, was dark. He was alone with these two.

"It's just us," said McGavin, seemingly reading Khoury's mind. "But Larry'll be joining us shortly. He's on his way over now. To meet us on his boat."

"Why?"

"Thought I'd help a fellow human being." McGavin smiled. He opened the passenger door and got out. Dave stood and began to walk over, his dreadlocks swinging. When Khoury didn't move, McGavin leant back inside and said, "Come on, then."

Dave opened Khoury's door. The only sound he could hear was of the waves beating against the outer wall, and the slap of ropes against masts in the wind. With a sense of foreboding, Khoury exited.

"Arms out," said Dave. He was wearing gloves too. When Khoury didn't comply, Dave lifted Khoury's arms so he was standing like a scarecrow. Dave patted him down, found the knife in an inside pocket, and removed it.

McGavin headed towards the harbour. Dave closed the car door and gave Khoury a shove so he followed McGavin, falling into step a few feet behind. McGavin stopped at the security gate in the fence. He tapped four numbers into the keypad. The gate unlocked with a metallic clunk, and they were inside the inner marina.

McGavin walked along the pontoon with purpose, like he belonged here. The boat was three sections along, at the end of a spur off the jetty. McGavin paused beside the boat for a moment, took in the lines. Khoury didn't need to read the name on the rear to know what it said. *The Etna, Ramsgate.*

The vessel rocked when McGavin stepped aboard. Khoury followed. He went over to where his brother Najjar had been stabbed, and bent down. The deck was scrubbed clean, no sign that someone had died there. When he turned around, McGavin was at the cabin door and Dave still on the pontoon, watching him.

McGavin unlocked the cabin and entered. Dave waited until Khoury followed. Stooping, Khoury went inside, his heart thumping. He wondered if he'd ever step out into the fresh air again alive. Then again, what was the purpose of existence without his family?

The interior was dimly lit by the spotlights outside, spilling in through netted portholes. It was cosy, just as he remembered. A tiny kitchen and table on either side of the gangway and further back a sleeping area. McGavin struck a match and held it to the wick of a hurricane lamp which hung on a strut overhead. The oil caught and McGavin blew out the match. He checked his watch.

"Sit down," he said. "I'll make us a cuppa while we're waiting on Larry." He opened a cupboard, took out a tea caddy, and put it on the work surface. He reached back inside and rummaged around. "Ah, there we are."

Three bags of white powder and a hammer joined the caddy.

IT WAS ANOTHER HALF an hour before Larry arrived. Khoury was alerted by a sudden tilt and footsteps on the hull.

His tea was half-drunk, gone cold. He was seated, facing the cabin door, McGavin standing nearby while Dave manned the galley kitchen, near the entrance.

Larry entered the cabin. He paused on the threshold, surprised to see Khoury. His eyes flicked to Dave. Khoury felt a surge of anger at the sight of his brother's murderer.

"You all right, Frank?" he asked.

"Come in," said McGavin.

Larry moved inside. Dave pulled the door to and stood in front of it. The space felt very constricted now.

"What are we going to do with him?" asked Larry.

"We?" said McGavin. "There's no we any more, Larry. You've been very stupid. The police know all about you. Which means they're coming to me."

"Sorry, I—"

"And there's this." McGavin held up the powder. "Selling drugs on the side?"

Larry gulped. Khoury could see his Adam's apple bobbing. Khoury was puzzled. Larry appeared to be in trouble, McGavin dealing with one of his own. "I'm just making a bit of extra money," said Larry.

"And running immigrants?"

"Two birds, one stone."

"More like three in this case. All you were supposed to do was deal with Regan."

"If everything had gone to plan you'd never have known."

"And that's supposed to make me feel better about it?"

Larry swallowed, clearly realising the stupidity of his admission. "Frank, I'm sorry. What can I do to make amends?"

"Nothing."

"I'll take the boat and disappear, how about it?"

"Good idea." McGavin nodded.

Without warning, Dave raised a claw hammer and struck Larry on the head. Larry tumbled to the floor as his legs gave way. Dave dropped the hammer, bent down, and rolled Larry over. Larry's breath was ragged. Khoury clenched his fists, his earlier foreboding rushing back.

Dave took a knife from a pocket. Khoury recognised it as his own. Dave held the knife out towards Khoury. Khoury didn't move, wondering if he were next. Coming to terms with what he was here for. Larry raised a hand, but Dave batted it away.

"Come on," urged Dave, gesturing with the knife once more. "Don't you want your revenge?"

Khoury decided he had no choice, it was clear he was going to die when it was over for Larry. Part of him was glad. Khoury accepted the weapon and stood over the wounded man.

"Please," whispered Larry. His eyes pleaded with Khoury, tears ran down his cheeks.

But Khoury was bereft of sympathy because, as his father used to say, when the calf falls, the knives come out. This man had killed his brother and probably his friend. He plunged the blade into Larry's chest over and over again until he was panting with the exertion. *This is for Najjar. This is for Shadid.* Covered in blood, Khoury paused. *This is for the life I will never be able to offer my family.*

Incredibly, Larry still struggled. He seemed to have the heart of an ox. Khoury raised his arms high and plunged the knife into Larry's stomach, as Larry had done to Najjar. Khoury leaned down on the handle, twisting the blade at the same time.

Larry groaned, his face distorted into a grimace of agony, head tilted back and straining. His fingers weakly scraped at the hilt. Khoury stared into Larry's face until he heaved a last breath and his eyes went blank. Khoury let out a huge breath.

"Feeling better?" asked McGavin.

Khoury didn't answer, he sat back on his haunches and stared at Larry's corpse. Khoury felt a calmness wash over him. He'd done what he needed – his vengeance was complete. He felt nothing for Larry, not pity, not hate. He was an empty shell now. And he suspected he was next.

"Dump him," said McGavin.

Dave took hold of Larry's clothes at the shoulders and dragged him outside. Khoury heard a splash as the corpse hit the water. Dave re-entered the cabin, picked up the hammer, and brought it over to Khoury.

"Take it," instructed McGavin. Khoury knew what they intended, though nothing mattered anymore. Khoury opened his fingers and allowed Dave to put the hammer in his palm. He closed his fist around it. There was blood and matted hair at the other end.

"See? That wasn't so hard. You can let go now." Khoury did so. Dave placed the hammer on the floor, just inside the door.

"Come on," said McGavin, pulling Khoury to his feet, a hand clamped around his arm. Khoury felt Najjar and Shadid either side of him. They would be with Khoury until the end.

Larry was floating next to the Etna, face down.

"I'll return Natalie's car," said Dave.

McGavin handed the keys over.

BURN THE EVIDENCE

Out on the jetty the sun was just rising, still nobody around. Khoury didn't care what was next. He enjoyed the warming rays on his face while McGavin led him away.

Thirty One

When the taxi began to move, Gray wound his watch forward an hour. The journey so far had thankfully proven uneventful. When he'd awoken this morning his throat still felt raw so he'd avoided eating. A drive to Dover, loading, a slow crossing of the North Sea, unloading, and a queue at Border Control, all on an empty stomach.

The whole way across, while the train whipped through the tunnel beneath the waves Gray hoped his sickness wouldn't occur again. He reflected that Tom had taken this same route, though on the water rather than below it. Gray was following in his footsteps, just far too late. He didn't trust himself to drive on the wrong side of the road, so he'd parked up on the French side and called a taxi.

The distance from the Eurotunnel terminal to Calais centre was short in comparison to the crossing and soon the taxi was pulling up at the Commissariat de Police on the corner of Place de Lorraine.

After handing over a few euros to the driver, Gray grabbed his briefcase and exited. The car was moving as soon as he closed the door. The station was a plain brown-brick building of a basic architecture which was typical of what he'd seen so far in Calais. No imagination had gone into the Post War construction. All the station's ground-floor windows were barred, two doors, in and out. A huge tricolour flapped overhead.

As Gray entered, he passed a uniformed cop talking on a mobile who paused briefly and eyed him. In the reception area, the décor was as uninspiring as the outside. He waited at the front desk until an administrator, a young woman wearing severe glasses, was available.

Gray showed his warrant card. "*Bonjour.* I'm here to see Inspector Morel. He's expecting me." Which wasn't true. He hadn't been able to reach Morel.

"Will he know what it is concerning?" she said.

"Yes."

"Okay, I will find him. Wait one moment, please."

"*Merci*," said Gray, now two thirds of the way through his back catalogue of French words. However, the administrator was already talking down a phone and missed his attempt at *entente cordiale*.

The woman covered up the mouthpiece with a hand. "Inspector Morel has no knowledge of your visit."

"I assure you, we communicated by email." Gray's message from yesterday had gone unanswered. "Inspector Morel sent me some files. I need to speak to him about them." He dug around in his bag for the paperwork and placed them on the desk before the administrator. She picked the pages up and flicked through them, then returned her attention to the phone, spoke briefly, and held the receiver out to Gray.

"Hello?"

"Sergeant Gray, how may I help you?" Morel's accent was thick. He pronounced Gray's name "Gree". In the background was an idling engine, raised voices, and an occasional gust of wind.

"It's about the bodies which washed up on our shores."

"Pardon?"

"Khoury, Najjar, and Shadid. You sent their files to me."

"Yes. You have them. Why are you here?"

"I was hoping you could fill in the blanks, Inspector Morel."

"Blanks? Ha! Of those there are many, Monsieur Gray. But I am a busy man."

"So am I, inspector. I came all the way from the UK to see you. I'm only here for a few hours before I get the train back."

"That was your decision."

"I would very much appreciate some of your time."

"It is not so far, the UK."

Gray said nothing, waited.

"Okay, I will give you a few moments. Although you will have to come and find me."

"Thank you. Where are you?"

"The Jungle, or what is left of it."

"I'll be with you soon." Gray wasn't going to give in. He handed the phone back to the administrator and asked her if she could order a taxi for him.

"It will be here shortly," she said.

THE DRIVER TOOK GRAY to the remnants of the Jungle on the eastern side of the Eurotunnel terminal and Calais itself. Gray had taken a circuitous route to find his man.

There was a small number of dull canvas constructions and a knot of people nearby. The group was composed of two opposing parties: immigrants and social workers, remonstrating with a handful of police, and several men in suits, probably local officials. Behind them, a bulldozer stood idling, its bucket pointed at the tents. A man sat in the bulldozer cab, chin in his hand, clearly bored. Beyond was a wire fence.

"Is this it?" asked Gray.

The driver nodded.

"Are you sure?"

"*Oui!*" Irritation was creeping into the driver's voice now.

Gray paid and got out, hearing shouting over the noise of the traffic running over the motorway above him. He made his way over, stepping carefully through rubbish strewn everywhere, trying to avoid the worst of the mud and puddles.

He hovered on the edge of the crowd, unnoticed, watching as a broad-shouldered man sporting an impressive moustache and glasses broke away from the group and walked over to the digger – unseen by the group intent on the slanging match. He crooked a finger at the man in the cab who leaned down, listened, and nodded. The driver, upright again, closed the cab door, revved his engine, and set off, aiming for the tents.

The arguing crowd paused; pointed fingers held in each other's faces. They looked over at the digger as it approached the tents, the migrants futilely waving their arms, trying to stop its progress. The argument forgotten, the disparate groups of protestors and police alike, dashed over, but too late. The driver ignored any protests and flattened one tent after another. The man with the moustache calmly walked back towards Gray while the two groups began rowing once more.

When the man was a few feet away Gray stopped him. "I'm looking for Inspector Morel."

The man didn't reply immediately, looking Gray up and down. Then he said, "Monsieur Gray?" Gray nodded. "I am

Morel." He stuck out a meaty hand for Gray to shake. "Call me Jacques. I am not keen on formality. My office said you were coming over."

"Then you must call me Solomon. What was all that about with the JCB?"

Morel sighed, the humour dropping away from his face. "A few months ago we cleared the Jungle and put a fence around it. We put the immigrants onto buses and moved them around the country. There were ten thousand of them at the time. And nearly a hundred more arriving every day, swelling an already big problem.

"Well, they keep coming back, trying to rebuild their shanty town. My men have to keep closing them down. The ones arguing," Morel nodded to the dejected group standing to one side with the immigrants, "they are social workers. But I have no choice. Orders are orders. Their town cannot be rebuilt."

"It sounds like an impossible task."

"Maybe." Morel brightened. "Come, let's get a coffee, talk about why you are here."

Morel led Gray back to a police car, the Frenchman careless of where he stepped as he sensibly wore wellington boots. Morel pointed to the passenger side, as Gray was about to get into the wrong side out of habit. In a couple of miles, Morel pulled into a petrol station and parked beside a truck. The sign on the wall outside said "Autogrill". Morel cut through the service area, past the tills, and outside onto a sunny terrace, crammed with people and tables, which faced fields.

"We have the choice of sitting or standing," said Morel. "Do you mind if we sit? I've been on my feet all day so far."

"Fine with me," said Gray. They took a table on the edge of the terrace.

Morel handed Gray a menu.

"I'm not hungry, thanks," said Gray. His stomach still wasn't feeling great.

"Are you sure? The food is very good here."

"Certain."

Morel perused the menu briefly, made a choice, and headed over to a counter to place his order. When Morel returned, he pulled out a packet of cigarettes, offered one to Gray which he declined, and lit up. Morel drew deeply on the stick and exhaled. The smoke was strong, acrid.

A waitress arrived at their table carrying a tray. Her hair was shaven close to her skull and her fingernails were painted black. She placed an espresso before Morel who spooned in a measure of sugar and stirred.

"What do you want to know?" asked Morel when she'd gone.

"About Khoury, Najjar, and Shadid."

"That is not easy. They were largely unfamiliar to us, Solomon. They kept their secrets well. It is not so unusual for people wanting a fresh start, to leave bad things behind. What we know was on the paper you received from me. I am sorry to say I have nothing more for you."

"You assumed they were from Syria."

"An educated guess," said Morel. "But we are pretty good at working out country of origin now. We have had plenty of practice." Morel laughed, although it was without humour.

"One of them, Khoury, had been accused of several crimes. Assault. Theft."

Morel shook his head sadly. "I was trying to persuade the man he allegedly beat to give evidence against him."

"Is he a local?"

"No, he lived in the Jungle too. He's gone now, shipped out during the rehousing. Animals, turning on their own."

"Does that happen a lot?"

"Who else are they going to take their frustrations out on?"

Lorry drivers and holiday makers, thought Gray.

"We had people undercover in the Jungle," said Morel, "and all they picked up was tiny pieces of information. Our trio spent all their time together, not mixing, barely speaking to anyone unless they had to. They were close. That's why we know so little. Then a few days ago they disappeared. We assumed they'd relocated to another area too."

"Maybe the UK?"

Morel shrugged. "Perhaps."

"And you had no thought of providing us with this information?"

"How were we to know for sure?"

"It's a decent assumption, though. With men like these, isn't safe better than sorry?"

"The trouble is, Solomon," said Morel flatly, "your government is only bothered by men like these, as you call them, when they become *your* problem. Most people I know have had nothing truly to do with the migrants. Usually they are just as frightened of us as we are of them. So many children separated from their parents. A long way from home and simply looking for a better life. They don't want to be here either. Those three though, they were the wolves. But we should not condemn the whole migration movement on the basis of a few bad people."

"Do you have access to any CCTV footage? To see how the men got out of the country?"

Morel snorted. "France is a liberal country so we spend very little time spying on our citizens. My men could investigate but it is best you assume we will not learn how and where they departed our shores for yours."

Gray picked up his briefcase and took out a file. "Do you recognise this man?" He slid over photo of Regan Armitage.

Morel leaned over and studied the face briefly. He shook his head. "I have never seen him before. Who is he?"

"We found him washed up with the other bodies."

"A smuggler then." Morel shrugged.

"We don't think so."

"But you are not sure?"

"No," admitted Gray. "What about this one?" It was an image of Larry Lost.

"Possibly. These men, though. They work in the shadows." Morel checked his watch. "I do not have long either, so if you want to ask anything else, now is the time."

Gray pulled out another photo. This time Morel picked it up, stared at the face for a long moment, and then raised his eyes to Gray's gaze.

"That's my son," said Gray. "He went missing just over ten years ago."

"I am sorry to hear that. What happened?"

"It's a long story. However, some new information came to light recently that he transited through Dover to Calais."

"Now I understand. This is why you are here."

"Not entirely."

Morel held up a hand. "I do not blame you. I have children, and I would go to the ends of the Earth to protect them. What can I do?"

"Could you search your records for any information on children brought through Calais around then?"

Morel pursed his lips. "That will not be easy."

"Please?"

"May I keep the photograph?"

"I can do better than that." Gray handed over a file. "These are some of his details."

The Frenchman flicked through the documents. "More than ten years you say?"

"I know, it's a long shot."

"But we have to try, yes?"

"Yes."

Morel checked his watch again. "Let me drive you to the Eurotunnel terminal," said Morel.

"You're busy, I can get a taxi."

"My car is just here. It is not much out of my way, and I'm happy to."

"Thanks."

Morel raced Gray along the roads in a stop-start process of rapid acceleration and sharp braking. He drew up outside the terminal a merciful few minutes later.

"Thank you, Jacques," said Gray. He held out a hand. Morel took it and shook.

"You are more than welcome. Call me if you need anything else." Morel handed over his business card. "My mobile number is on there. Then you have a better chance of catching me."

Gray got out, and Morel screeched away.

While Gray waited to board he considered his morning's work. In terms of the Regan case Gray hadn't learned a great deal more from Morel. However, it appeared there was nothing to know. Regan was anonymous in Calais. There seemed to be no connection between him and people smuggling. So what was his link to the immigrants?

Most importantly though, Gray now had a contact in France, someone who maybe cared and seemed to want to help finding Tom. The investigation to find his missing son was back on again.

And tomorrow he had a funeral to attend.

Thirty Two

Gray picked up the voicemail when he turned his phone back on. The train was emerging from the tunnel back in the UK, and he had a signal again. He rang Hamson from his car.

"How are you feeling?" she asked. A seagull squawked overhead.

"Not great, thanks for asking."

"I'm sorry to do this but I need you here. Larry Lost has been found."

"Ha ha, very funny Von."

"He's dead."

Gray swore. "How? Where?"

"He was stabbed and dumped in Ramsgate harbour. When can you get here?"

"I'll be as fast as I can."

"Thanks."

GRAY PARKED OUTSIDE the maritime museum on the Ramsgate harbour, just beyond the stone needle monument. He showed his warrant card to a uniform on the perimeter cordon and ducked underneath the tape. He made his way to the tightest concentration of people and found Hamson there, blowing on a steaming polystyrene cup.

"You took your time," she said, peeling away from the conversation she'd been having.

"What do we know?" asked Gray.

Hamson tilted her head to say "follow me" and led Gray through a gate in a fence which ran around the harbour edge. He stepped onto a wooden pontoon which bobbed gently underfoot. Hamson took him to the end and along a spur. She stopped beside the Etna.

"The owner of another boat found Larry floating face down out there." Hamson pointed towards the middle of the harbour, a channel which the boats would navigate to make their way in and out. "He called us straight away."

"How long had he been immersed?"

"Clough reckons at least half a day. He probably drifted very slowly out. Divers are down there now, searching the bottom."

"Was he dead when he went in?"

Hamson shrugged. "You know what Clough's like, he's not keen to commit either way. But it's a safe bet. Larry had had the back of his head smashed and multiple stab wounds. We found the hammer inside the cabin, next to the door." She pointed at the Etna. "You should take a look inside."

Gray put on overshoes and nitrile gloves given to him by one of the SOCOs working aboard. Hamson didn't follow, she'd seen it already. The cabin area was cramped. Gray crouched at the entrance. There was just about enough room for three SOCOs to work in the galley if they were careful.

There was no need for Gray to go any further. Blood was everywhere, a particularly large pool just beneath him. It smelt like a butcher's shop. SOCOs had put metal plates down on the deck so they could walk back and forth without disturbing the evidence. The place where the hammer had been found was identified with a yellow plastic marker. Leading from the pool to Gray, was a wide smear which continued to the gunwale.

"What do you think?" asked Hamson when he returned.

"Appears he was stabbed in the galley, then dragged out and thrown overboard."

"Agreed. We found glass on the floor and a mug with a half-drunk cup of tea. So it appears somebody broke in and awaited Larry's arrival. There's fingerprints we're analysing."

A mass of bubbles broke the water's surface and Hamson's flow. One of the divers rose up. In his hand he held a knife.

Thirty Three

It had been a long twenty-four hours. Gray had managed to grab a little sleep, then he was up again and into the station for an early briefing. Gray felt a shadow of himself. The hammer had been a major discovery. However, it was what forensics didn't find that was troubling – the ketamine was gone, though Gray had to keep this to himself. He could hardly admit to an illegal search of what was a major crime scene a few hours later.

Hamson held the floor, giving a brief update on the latest findings, and doling out the actions. "Early evening yesterday, Larry Lost, a known associate of Frank McGavin, was found face down in Ramsgate harbour. Early indications are, he was hit on the back of the head with a hammer then stabbed, before being dumped overboard. We found both murder weapons, one inside the boat, the other in the water.

"Based on findings by forensics, it appears someone waited for the victim to turn up on his boat before attacking him. A mug of tea was found. The fingerprints on the mug match those on the knife and hammer. They belong to Adnan Khoury.

"We also know that Larry was looking for Khoury. Larry, and another as yet unidentified male, searched the Lighthouse Project two nights ago. It appears Khoury got to Larry first.

"Additionally, we've received the test results from the blood analysis on Najjar and Shadid. Neither showed any signs of ingesting ketamine, meaning it was Regan alone who'd taken the narcotic.

"Turning to actions. Mike, as Sol is going to Regan's funeral, you get the PM on Larry. CCTV needs checking out around the harbour. What time did Khoury arrive? How did he get there?" A DC volunteered for the work.

"What about the blue wig?" asked Gray. "Any progress in tracking down anywhere that sells hairpieces locally?"

"Mike?" said Hamson.

"Several places deal with rugs, but not the type we're looking for. There's nowhere on Thanet applicable. I even tried the joke shops and fancy dress shops. Nothing."

"Did you go any further afield?" asked Gray.

"There's Independence Hair in Canterbury but they don't do blue."

"Nowhere else?"

"Do you want me to call every shop in the bloody country?" implored Fowler.

"It could have been bought over the internet," said Hamson.

"Which would be near impossible to tackle."

"Mike's right, Sol. Looks like this is a dead end at the moment."

"What about the CCTV from Seagram's? Have you had chance to look over it again?"

"Not yet."

"Let's move on," said Hamson. She handed out several more items before Gray could excuse himself, head to the toilets, and put his tie on, ready for the funeral.

THE FUNERAL DIRECTOR'S was on the edge of Margate. Gray's old double-breasted suit wasn't robust enough to keep out the chill. It was the required black, however. He shoved his hands deeper into his pockets. The temperature had to be low because this was where the bodies were stored. Or, more accurately, displayed, in the chapel of rest: some old stable buildings constructed of stone, out the back away from the office and across a courtyard.

The last time he'd done this it was to say goodbye to Nick Buckingham. Different room, different mortician, same objective.

Regan lay in a coffin located in the centre of the square room, raised up on trestles, angled slightly so the head was above the feet. Arrangements of yellow blooms in the corners and plain brick walls painted white gave the space a sterile touch. Lilies again.

The coffin itself was a money-no-object affair constructed of burnished timber, something like oak, a dense, high-quality wood; six gold handles; and an inscribed gold plate atop the lid, which itself was propped up against a wall because the casket was open for now.

Regan was dressed in a white open-neck shirt and tan chinos, hands clasped across his chest. He appeared to be asleep, a peaceful expression on his face, which had been well tended by the undertaker. No outward sign of Clough's intrusion during the post mortem. There was a hint of colour on the cheeks, and the lips were upturned in a suggestion of contentment. Ruffled white silk lined the interior.

"It's time," said the undertaker standing in the doorway behind him.

"It's always somebody's time," replied Gray.

THE CREMATORIUM WAS located on the long, straight Manston Road which connected Margate with the old air force base, now renamed Kent International Airport, except nothing took off from its runway anymore, and even back when it had, "international" just meant Jersey. Yet another failed local business venture where only weeds were successful.

The crematorium itself was braced by St Mildred's Catholic school and the local refuse tip. Across the road were cabbage fields and the Margate skyline.

Gray indicated, turned into the crematorium, and wound his way along the twisty tarmac drive. Usually parking was a challenge, and cars could often be found shoved all along the narrow route. The legitimate spaces filled quickly because services ran in succession. As one finished and the mourners filed out the back, a new lot headed in through the front.

Today was a rarity; the parking spaces were mainly empty. Which probably meant an older person's life was currently being celebrated. As you aged, fewer people were willing and able to see you off. Friends and family tended to whittle away over the years. That would not be the case for Regan. His would be a throng. It usually was for the young.

Gray picked a spot adjacent to the drive, backing into the gap so he was facing the right direction, positioned to minimise the queuing on the way out. He locked the car and made his way over to the low-slung, single-storey red-brick-built crematorium over which tall chimneys towered.

Double doors of wood and metal led into a hallway, offices left and right. In front, duplicate doors allowed access to the auditorium. However, they were firmly closed. Standing a few feet away, Gray could clearly hear the service underway. He retreated outside once more.

If he had been smoking still, now would be the perfect time to light up, to obtain that fleeting internal warmth. Instead, Gray made a circuit of the building and entered the memorial garden at the rear. There were bouquets and flower arrangements, fresh and dewed. This was the exit, the final act in the funereal process where the attendees would be funnelled, manoeuvred by the crematorium staff like shoppers being managed through a retail experience, the route to follow, subtly obvious.

The path was a dogleg of flagstones leading from the building to the car park via budding rose bushes and brass plaques to the dead. Gray idled in the garden for a few minutes, examining the floral displays and reading the panels. The hum of organ music and voices in song floated out; a hymn Gray recognised but could not name. Then it too petered out, leaving the sound of a plane flying overhead.

Gray was considering retracing his steps when the doors sprung open. A besuited man stepped into the garden, closely followed by an old lady in black. She stopped, stared at Gray in surprise. He was an interloper. Gray retreated. The car park had begun to fill.

Gray found the auditorium was open now. The echoic expanse contained some of Gray's fellow mourners. Rectangular in dimension, a central aisle cut through parallel rows of benches. There were wide margins either side for standing space. At the fore, a kind of stage was towered over by high, stained-glass windows. To the right, at an alignment of approximately one o'clock, was a pulpit; and at three o'clock, doors of identical design to the others. This was the exit into the gardens, squaring Gray's circular journey.

The architectural scheme was all things to all people. Subtly ecclesiastical, sufficient to appeal to the God-fearing, while suitably unadorned to appease the agnostics. This wasn't a church but it could be a place of worship, if so desired. Gray took a spot at the back at the end of the bench, the point furthest from the pulpit. He wasn't here to grieve; he was here because Jake had asked.

What was initially a trickle of people, soon became a biblical flood. The available seats filled from forward to back, with just the very front row left vacant for immediate family. All bore downcast expressions. No celebration of life, this. Carslake entered. He took a spot halfway down.

The low hum of discussion steadily increased as voices fought to be heard. Five minutes before the service was due to start, the auditorium was full to bursting; all the standing room taken. Even the hall outside was packed. Regan hadn't been a popular person, the mourners would be here for Jake, to show respect because he was an important man with influence in local society. Gray frowned when Frank McGavin entered. Carslake noted him too, his eyes following McGavin's progress.

McGavin walked along the central aisle to the second row. A couple of men stood up, creating a gap for McGavin. They moved away towards the rear. His people, reserving a space for the dignitary.

"May I?" Gray shifted his attention away from McGavin. It was Natalie from the Lighthouse, dressed in a dark, knee-length skirt, a white blouse which rode high on the neck, and a jacket which matched the skirt.

Gray slid a couple of inches along the bench to allow Natalie to perch beside him. There wasn't really the space. He felt hemmed in, sandwiched between Natalie and an older man he didn't know, who frowned at the intrusion. He breathed in a faint wash of a flowery perfume from one direction and the musky odour of deodorant from the other.

"Thank you," she said. "Here on police business?"

"Partially. What about you?"

"Everybody knows the Armitages, right?"

Before Gray could reply, a silence drifted across the auditorium. Everyone stood and turned to watch the coffin's slow progress down the aisle. There were six pallbearers, including Cameron. Jake walked behind the coffin, his head raised, eyes forward, being strong outwardly, probably crumbling within.

They carried the casket the length of the auditorium, then slowly levered it from their shoulders before lowering it onto a garlanded dais. Role completed, the bearers retreated, except Cameron who slipped onto the front row followed by Jake. The silence remained utter.

At the pulpit stood a woman. Gray hadn't noticed her enter. She must have done so while attention was on the procession. She was dressed in a dark blue trouser suit; dark hair tied back, no make-up, unremarkable in every way. She would not be upstaging the service.

"Good morning everyone," she said in a steady, clear voice. "On behalf of the family, I welcome you. My name is Caroline Villers. Today we have come together to celebrate the life of Regan C Armitage, cruelly cut short in tragic circumstances.

"I have spent time with the family to better get to know Regan as we have only met in death. I learnt that even though Regan's time on earth was too short, it was filled with joy, and during which he had a positive impact on so many people's lives. That the auditorium is full today is visual proof.

"We are here to say goodbye, to express the love we all bear for Regan and the regard in which we held and still hold him. Regan was not religious and neither is his family, so I have been asked by Regan's father, Jake, to conduct a Humanist ceremony. There is a poem which I felt was apt." She paused a second before speaking out over the crowd, citing the verse from memory.

There were some sniffles from the mourners, several tears too. Throughout the poem Jake nodded, the words obviously meaning much to him.

"Regan was a son, a brother and, most of all, a friend," continued Villers. "He was a man who enjoyed life and shared his time with many people. He was a son of Margate; born at the hospital just a few miles away and lived in the area his whole life, so it is fitting that he ends his time here too." Another brief pause. "Now, Regan's father, Jake, would like to say a few words."

Villers stepped back a few feet to allow Jake to take her place at the lectern. He pulled a sheaf of paper from his inside pocket, placed it on the pulpit, and spent a few moments smoothing it out while he composed himself. He eyed the coffin and spoke directly to his dead son while he read a poem.

When he'd finished, Jake lifted his head up from the paper. His eyes made a sweep of the room of assembled mourners. The silence stretched. Some shifted in their seats as time moved on.

"At times like this we are not supposed to speak ill of the dead. But none of you really knew Regan. He was a damaged boy who struggled to connect with people on anything more than a basic level. He was troubled and suffered bouts of depression. Many here, though, will be aware of Regan's regular social events. You'll think he was a bundle of fun.

"It was a sham, though. Regan couldn't connect with a cat. He did some terrible things over the years, which I, to my shame, shut my eyes and ears to."

Natalie turned her head to Gray and raised her eyebrows. He was one of several mourners shifting in their seats; a few even shaking their heads.

"But he was my son." Jake raised the paper, scrunched it up, "I am not comforted. I am angry, I am vengeful! I will find out who was involved in my son's death and I *will* deliver justice. Whoever you are, I will hunt you down. This I swear." Jake dropped the paper onto the floor and returned to his seat. He stared resolutely forward, ignoring the chatter which erupted after a moment's shocked silence.

"Oh my God," whispered Natalie. But Gray wasn't listening. Instead he was keeping his attention on McGavin who leaned forward and placed a reassuring hand on Jake's shoulder.

Villers bent down to retrieve Jake's poem from the floor, folded it, and put it inside her jacket. She used the pulpit for apparent support, not quite sure what to say at this unusual turn of events. Her mouth opened and closed several times as she fought for words.

Eventually, Villers gathered her wits and spoke loudly in an attempt to restore order, "At this point we will spend a minute or two remembering Regan's part in our lives, the good times and the sad times, the funny times, the special times. When you are ready then please move through to the memorial garden." Villers hastily opened the doors, propping them back by locking them top and bottom, and exited herself. It seemed she couldn't get out fast enough although no one else moved, perhaps too keen to witness the next spectacle, whatever it might be.

Jake stood, giving the signal for the mourners to depart. Keeping his back turned to everyone, Jake crossed to his son's coffin.

"Excuse me," said Gray to Natalie.

"Of course, sorry." Natalie headed for the main doors and the car park.

As Gray neared, Jake stretched out a hand, placed a palm on the wooden surface of the coffin, where his son's head would be. Only when Jake's hand dropped away did Gray speak. "I'm sorry for your loss."

"Thank you," replied Jake though he didn't turn around. "You'll be coming to the wake at Seagram's then. Join me in a toast."

"I don't think I can."

"It wasn't a question."

Gray was in a dilemma, go or not? Hamson had warned him of getting too close to Jake, and here he was, considering going.

"There's free booze."

"I'm on the wagon."

"There's free orange juice."

"I'm not supposed to ..."

"To what?" Now Jake twisted at the waist, brought eyes to bear on Gray. "Speak to me?"

"Something like that."

"Times like these are when you need your friends."

"Then as a friend let me advise you not to make threats in public."

"It was a fact, not a threat. So what?"

"Let me and my colleagues do our jobs."

"And when your son disappeared, did you sit back, and let someone else take control?"

Gray was on thin ice. He'd carried on looking for Tom, regardless of what else was going on around him. "All I'll ask is that if you learn anything share it with me before you do something about it."

"Deliver a swift justice, you mean?"

"Your words, not mine."

Jake stared at Gray for a moment. "See you at Seagram's." Then he left.

NATALIE WAS STANDING in the car park, smoking an e-cigarette as was all the rage these days. Gray smelt strawberry mint. The exodus was in full flow. Cars streaming away from the crematorium, creating a localised traffic jam as they attempted to turn right across the busy road, back to Margate.

"That was ... unique," said Natalie.

"A new one on me," said Gray. "Are you a friend of the family?"

Natalie shrugged. "I just wanted to be here."

Gray wondered why. There was no apparent connection between her and the Armitages.

"What about you? Here in an official or unofficial capacity?"

"Both."

"What about the wake? Or is it straight back to the station for you?"

"I wasn't intending to. You?"

She shook her head. "I don't think I'd be entirely welcome. Can I get a lift back to the Lighthouse? It's only round the corner from Seagram's. I got the bus then walked here, and now my feet are killing me." Natalie leaned against a car, removed a shoe, and massaged a foot to emphasise the point. "I'd really appreciate it."

Gray felt like he couldn't say no, though for some reason part of him screamed to do so. "Sure," he said.

An old couple stopped beside Gray. "Excuse me," the man said to Natalie. "That's my car you're leaning against."

"Sorry," said Natalie. She put her shoe back on and moved out of their way.

"I'm over here," said Gray.

"That was awkward," she whispered.

He unlocked his car, motioned for Natalie to get in. Gray started his engine and pulled out of the spot. He paused while Regan's funeral cortege passed by. Jake stared at Gray, seeing Natalie. His expression hardened, and he turned away. Gray pulled out and followed the black limousine.

The few miles of the journey occurred in silence. As Gray drove towards Margate he could see a pall of grey smoke rising over the town. When they reached the Lighthouse Natalie thanked him again, got out of his car, and went inside without a backward glance.

Gray drove the rest of Belgrave Road. Out of curiosity at the junction he turned towards the New Town rather than to Seagram's. He slowed and looked along the pedestrianised shopping area. A few hundred yards along were a couple of fire engines and an ambulance. Gray bumped the car up a kerb, stuck on the hazard lights, and followed the blue flashing lights.

Thirty Four

Carslake found Jake at the bar, alone in a cast of many, empty stools either side. Carslake took one of them.

"What'll you have?" asked Jake.

"As you're paying, a single malt."

Jake offered a thin smile to Carslake and said to the barman hovering a few feet away, "Get him the good stuff."

"Yes, Mr Armitage."

"Look at this lot." Jake nudged his chin at the reflections in the mirror behind the bar. "Drowning their sorrows. It's not them who's lost a son."

People were stuffing their faces with Jake's food, consuming alcohol in eye-watering quantities. Mostly it appeared opportunistic. The chance of a free feeding and watering being literally grabbed with both hands.

"They've lost a friend, though." Carslake thought of Cameron. "And one of them a brother."

"Friends," snorted Jake. "I don't even know who half of them are." Just then, a couple came over and offered Jake condolences. He acknowledged them with a brief nod.

The whisky arrived in a heavy tumbler. "Ice or water, sir?" asked the barman.

"Just a splash of water, please."

The barman dribbled in some water and handed Carslake the tumbler. He raised the glass towards Jake.

"A toast. Here's to Regan. May he be at peace."

"*Slainte*," replied Jake. They clinked glasses and drank. The whisky slid down too easily.

"Want another?" asked Jake, crooking his finger at the barman who was obviously there to service Jake and nobody else.

Carslake was tempted but said, "I'm driving."

"You can walk back to the station from here."

"Turning up pissed wouldn't be a good idea."

"That Inspector. Hamson, is it? She keeping an eye on you?"

"She's one of the good ones."

"A taxi back home then. Your car will be safe enough here."

"I'll take the orange juice. Plenty of ice this time."

"Another for me too." A double whisky with a pint of lager. "No matter how hard I try I can't seem to get drunk. And I've been trying very hard for some time now."

The soft drink arrived and Carslake took a sip.

"Do you believe in God?" asked Jake.

Carslake wasn't surprised. He decided on honesty for once. "No and I never have."

"Me neither, though I'm beginning to wonder now."

"Oh?"

"Whether all this is retribution from on high."

Carslake didn't have an answer for Jake, nobody did.

"You look like shit, my friend." Frank McGavin sat at a bar stool, leaned around Jake, and nodded at Carslake. "Good to see you."

Carslake raised an eyebrow, said nothing in reply.

"Have one with me," said Jake.

"That's why I'm here," said McGavin. Carslake was surprised to hear him order gin.

When the drink had been delivered to McGavin he raised his glass in a toast. "To loss. May it make us stronger."

Jake reciprocated, uttered no words of his own. Carslake didn't pick up his glass.

McGavin shook his head ruefully. "I can't believe it. He was too young." He placed a hand on Jake's shoulder. "You have my best wishes. And call me, at any time, day or night, should you need anything. I mean anything. The police have their uses but I can be more effective." McGavin winked at Carslake.

When McGavin had disappeared into the crowd, Carslake said, "Frank McGavin, should I be worried?"

"McGavin likes to make out we're friends."

"Are you?"

"This sounds very much like you're questioning me, Chief Inspector."

"Maybe I am. You should be careful who you keep close."

"I told you, it's nothing." Jake had another large drink.

Carslake didn't know how to respond. "I'd better be going." He stood up. "Again, my condolences."

Carslake left Jake staring at the slowly melting ice cubes in his glass.

Thirty Five

What had been the offices of *Thanet's Voice* was now blown-out windows and blackened bricks. It appeared the fire had been mainly confined to Noble's residence. The buildings either side – a charity shop and a cash converter – and the Chinese takeaway below were largely untouched. The smell of smoke was thick in the air.

Gray stood aside as a fire engine drove away, leaving one remaining on site. At the cordon, Gray showed his warrant card, asked for whoever was in charge. The uniform pointed towards a fireman clad in fluorescent gear standing in the shadow of the engine with two of his colleagues. Gray walked over and introduced himself.

"Marchmont," said the fireman in response. He looked Gray up and down. "Been to a funeral?"

"Yes."

"Oh, sorry."

"I was passing by. Have you been in yet?" asked Gray.

"Just about to. The blaze was set by the time we arrived. All we could do was put it out before it spread. What's your interest?"

"The person who lives here has been involved in a case I'm investigating."

"Wouldn't surprise me, knowing William Noble," said Marchmont.

"Can I take a look?"

"As long as you stay with me."

Gray followed Marchmont down the alley. The door to Noble's flat stood open. The vent which usually spewed out hot air from the takeaway was silent. The aroma of Chinese food was replaced by the stench of burned wood and plastic. Marchmont led Gray up the stairs. The Chief stopped Gray on the small landing. "This is as far as you go."

Gray leaned inside the single room which opened off the landing. Gray coughed, the residual fumes getting into his lungs. On the far side of the space was another doorway to the second area. There were firemen in there too. The flames had scorched every surface.

"Can you smell that?" said Marchmont.

Gray sniffed. Clearly Marchmont expected Gray to detect something over the burning. "Petrol?"

"Well done, Sergeant."

"So the fire was deliberate?"

"That would be my assumption."

"Sir!" A shout from one of Marchmont's men. He beckoned Marchmont from the back room. Marchmont disappeared inside for a few minutes. Gray stood impatiently, keen to know what they'd found. The Chief returned, a grim expression on his face.

"There's a corpse," he said.

"I need to see."

"It's not pretty."

"I'll survive."

Marchmont led Gray through, pointing out where to put his feet. Crammed into the corner of the back room, by a window, was the charred remains of a person. By the size of the body it appeared to be Noble, but the white hair was gone, as was most of the clothes revealing blackened skin like a piece of chicken overcooked on a barbecue. The sight made Gray feel like throwing up. But he made himself go over. There was the gold ring. It was Noble for sure.

"I'll get forensics," said Gray.

Gray pulled out his mobile and went downstairs to make the call in the fresh air. Before he could do so his mobile rang. It was the custody sergeant, Morgan. "Got a lad in one of the interview rooms we've just arrested, says wants you."

"Who is it?"

A pause while Morgan flicked over a page, the sound loud down the phone. "Ray Quigley, tattoos everywhere. Know him?"

"I'll be there shortly. Look after Quigley for me, will you?"

"He isn't going anywhere," said Morgan and disconnected.

William Noble only had one more journey to make. To the mortuary. There was nothing more Gray could do.

Thirty Six

First, Gray went to his desk, took off his jacket, and hung it over the back of his chair. He sat down and pulled his keyboard over. He wanted to carry out some research into Quigley before they met. Five minutes, and he had what he wanted. Gray called Morgan and asked him to bring Quigley through from his cell.

When Gray entered the interview room, Quigley was staring at the table. He wouldn't meet Gray's eye. His body was folded in on itself, shoulders hunched. The impact of the folder onto the melamine surface made Quigley jerk. He wasn't looking in the slightest like someone who wanted to be here.

Gray dragged out a chair, made the legs scrape. He sat down, hands in trouser pockets, open body language, in contrast to Quigley's. He paused. Gray had all the time in the world whereas the pressure would be building on Quigley.

"What's going on, Ray?"

Quigley didn't acknowledge the question, kept his eyes downcast. Gray didn't mind, he turned his attention to the file he'd brought in, flipped it open, and read. "Says here you've been charged with dealing Class A drugs. Pretty stupid as you've prior for possession, carrying cannabis."

"That was for personal use."

"Which is why you only got community service. Seems like you've moved up a league, though. Dealing now?" He fixed

Quigley with a knowing look. "And it's your second offence. Up to fourteen years if you get a judge with something to prove. We've been cracking down recently." Gray closed the file. "Why did you ask for me?"

"I want to come to an arrangement. I've got information."

Gray let the scepticism show in his face and voice. "Yeah, right."

"I do!"

"I'm not in the drug squad." Gray rose from his seat. "I'll get one of my colleagues; they can manage you better than I can."

"It's about Regan."

Gray paused, sat back down again. "Go on." He was intrigued but suspected it would turn out to be nothing; that Quigley was desperate and would say anything to keep him here. "I'm listening."

Quigley shook his head. "Not until you promise I won't be done for dealing. No recordings, no solicitors. This is between me and you. Cos if this gets out I won't be walking straight again. Ever."

Gray sat back, thought about the proposition and about Quigley. In the silence, Quigley began to fidget. He blinked repeatedly and he appeared to be talking to himself, his mouth moving but no words to be heard. Panicking more about doing a stretch than whoever would take him out, Gray assumed.

"I want to hear what you've got before I decide," said Gray.

"I'm not happy about that."

"That's what's on offer, Ray."

It was Quigley's turn to sit back and consider. He was talking to himself again, his leg jigging up and down rapidly. Whatever was inside was bottled up firmly. He was steeling himself. Getting ready for the battle ahead. The battle with his conscience.

"Okay, I'll talk," said Quigley eventually.

"I'm listening."

"Regan wasn't all he seemed."

"Tell me something I don't know. Nobody ever is, and his father said so openly at his funeral."

"Not like this, though. I knew him pretty well. He was a right piece of work. We had to make sure he got looked after, had what he wanted, when he wanted it."

"He's the boss's son, you said so yourself, I remember."

"Sure, but there are limits, you know?"

"Such as?"

"He had to get served the moment he reached the bar."

"Annoying, yes, though what does that matter? You said it was just a job."

"Do you know how much shit I take for letting someone queue jump?"

"You're not giving me anything here that's of use, Ray."

"He used the club to trawl for women."

"And other men don't?"

"We had a couple of incidents." Quigley trailed off.

"Like what?"

Quigley stayed mute. Seemingly this was his Rubicon. Cross and there was no going back. Gray repeated his question.

"Trying it on with girls who were too drunk to say no. It got hushed up each time."

"By who?" When Quigley didn't answer, once more Gray asked, "By his father?"

"Regan's mistakes had a habit of going away."

"How?"

"The girls got paid off."

"Do you know that for sure?"

Quigley shifted in his seat. "Not for sure, no. It was just something Regan said, about being untouchable."

"Is there anyone who can corroborate your story?"

Quigley snorted out a laugh. "Unlikely."

Gray made a mental note to look into this a little more. Maybe someone had been into the station and made a complaint. A long shot, but you never knew. He changed tack. "What happened the night Regan disappeared?"

"He was in the club, as usual. Coming to the bar a lot. Of course, as the manager I had to serve him. He liked that, showing who was really the boss. There were some who bent to him, thinking that one day Regan would inherit, and he'd do them favours. No chance. The man was a snake."

"I think we've established you didn't like Regan. I need something more specific."

"He was with a woman."

"What did she look like?"

"Tall. Blue hair."

"Anything else?"

"That was all I saw. She was by the dance floor. The lights were bright, and I was busy. Not much chance to kick back and take in the sights. It's all booze, booze, booze."

"What was Regan on?"

"His special beer. She had wine."

"That's it?"

Quigley shook his head. Reluctance crept in once again.

"This is all supposition so far," said Gray. "There's no evidence."

"He bought other stuff."

"What?"

"Drugs."

"Which?"

Quigley wouldn't answer. Gray repeated his question.

"Ketamine."

Gray considered this. "Serious stuff." Three incidences of the drug now, all seemingly related to Regan.

"I passed it over with the second round of drinks."

"What's the purpose of ketamine?"

"It's a relaxant."

"It makes whoever takes it compliant?"

Quigley shrugged. "Maybe."

"Was it for his own use?"

Quigley laughed. "Regan didn't do drugs."

"Never?"

"No, he said drugs were for idiots."

Gray thought about the ketamine in Regan's blood sample.

"So he only gave drugs to other people?" said Gray.

Quigley nodded. "That's right."

"Sounds very much to me that you were aiding and abetting another one of Regan's 'incidents'."

"I had nothing to do with it! I just sold him gear. It was up to him what happened next. You've got to believe me."

"Had Regan bought drugs from you before?"

"Once or twice. If there was someone he was keen on, but the woman wasn't quite so interested then he'd buy."

"What then, once he had the drugs?"

Quigley shrugged. "He didn't come back to the bar. I assumed he'd left with her like before. To use the gear, I'd have bet."

"What did you think when he wound up dead?"

"It was a complete surprise. I never thought he'd go that way."

"Did you care?"

"About Regan?" Quigley laughed. "He was only interested in himself so why would I be bothered about him?"

"That's cold, Ray."

Another shrug. "He's dead."

"Who did you buy the ketamine from?"

"I suppose it doesn't matter now. He's dead too. My supplier was Larry Lost."

"Anything else you'd like to add? Now's the time."

Quigley shook his head. Gray stood. So did Quigley.

"Where do you think you're going?" asked Gray.

"I'm leaving."

"Whatever gave you that idea?"

"You said we had an agreement."

"They were your words, not mine. Separately, you admitted to an additional charge of dealing in Seagram's, and you hindered a murder investigation by not coming forward with this latest information, which is obstruction."

"You bastard!" Quigley stepped forward. His muscles bulged as he clenched his fists. If he swung, Gray would be in trouble. Gray kept the table between them and his hand on a chair in case he had to use it.

"You want to add assaulting an officer to the charges?" asked Gray, his tone a lot calmer than he felt.

Quigley seethed. He was breathing deeply, like a bull about to charge. Then he flopped back down into his seat. "You promised," he said.

"I didn't promise anything." Gray opened the door, said as he was leaving, "No recording, no evidence. That's what you wanted, wasn't it?"

Thirty Seven

Then

The room was small. It seemed to be an office. There was a desk and some photographs. The central heating pipes knocked as water gurgled through them. Otherwise there was just a female police constable to keep Rachel company. She said her name was Karen.

Karen had been very nice so far, offering Rachel drinks and food. But Rachel wasn't hungry or thirsty. Karen had also tried to engage in conversation, but Rachel had nothing to say either. All that interested Rachel was her father and brother. Rachel wanted them here so they could all go home.

The detective who'd loaned her his jacket, Jeff, she remembered, knocked, and entered. He said something quietly to Karen, who stood up, surrendering the chair.

"Can I join you?" he asked Rachel. She nodded. Jeff brought Karen's chair nearer, but left some distance between them. He sat down. "How are you?"

"Where's my dad?" said Rachel. "When's he coming?"

Jeff stared at her, his expression neutral. "I'm sorry to say I have some bad news."

Rachel's bottom lip began to quiver, not wanting to believe what she knew deep down was coming next. "Is my dad dead?"

"I'm very sorry, Rachel. It was the smoke."

"Can I see him?"

"I wouldn't advise you to do that."

"What about my brother?"

Jeff shook his head. "Do you know where your mother is?"

Rachel sucked in a lungful of air, unable to speak, her chest about to burst with grief. Her head dipped, tears began to flow down her cheeks, dripping onto her lap. She felt utterly lost and alone, entirely unsure what to do next. Although she'd always been independent, this was a whole new world for her.

"There's someone waiting to see you," said Jeff. Rachel didn't react, she couldn't.

"Hello, Rachel, I'm a social worker, and my name is Tiffany."

Rachel forced herself to look up. She didn't look like a Tiffany. A kindly, middle-aged woman, her hair in a pixie cut, smiled at Rachel in a mix of pleased-to-see-her tinged with sadness. Rachel recognised her type. She'd been in care before.

"We've been trying to find your aunt so she can come and get you but I'm sorry to say she's on holiday in the Canary Islands."

"So what happens now?" asked Rachel.

"We need to find you somewhere to live until your aunt returns."

"A home?"

"Yes, it might be a few days or a bit more. I'm sorry I can't be exact."

Rachel didn't care what happened. She was alone and lost.

"Would you mind coming with me?" asked Tiffany.

Rachel stood up. As she passed Jeff she handed back his jacket. He smiled at her, put a hand on her shoulder.

"Everything will be okay," he said.

But Rachel knew he was lying.

Thirty Eight

N**ow** Gray found Hamson in the detective's office.

"Have you heard about William Noble?" she asked him.

"I arrived at his office when they found him. There's more." He brought Hamson up to date regarding Quigley's confession.

"Larry seems to be our connection to everything," said Hamson. "He was at the Lighthouse trying to find Khoury, beat up Noble, sold Quigley drugs."

"And now Noble's dead."

"We've all been singularly unsuccessful at tracking down Adnan Khoury. He seems to have disappeared off the face of the earth."

"I reckon your old mate's in all this."

"With Khoury?"

Hamson shook her head. "Noble. Burning the evidence. That's Jake's game, isn't it?"

"We're hardly mates, not any more. Noble told me he was investigating some bunch called Millstone."

"Who?"

"Developers." Gray got the protest flier from the march and handed it to Hamson. She looked it over. "And somehow McGavin is involved. He's been buying up property as well. Larry Lost worked for Frank."

"So Noble's sniffing around got him killed?"

"Maybe."

"Over houses?"

"People have died due to stranger things. I need to do a bit of digging into the files, see if anyone made a complaint about Regan." And while he was in the files he'd look at the Sunset fire too, something else Noble had mentioned.

"You can do that later; first we're paying Frank McGavin a visit."

FRANK MCGAVIN WAS REPUTED to possess many material items: money, houses, people, and a stable of horses. He was the man who wanted for nothing. Control was his thing; primarily over supply chains and routes to market for illicit and illegal activities, people too.

According to Noble, McGavin's physical portfolio had recently expanded to include a restaurant called Fruits de Mer, which commanded a marine view on the Broadstairs cliff top, providing upmarket seafood. Inside Gray found it to be understated yet tastefully decorated. Pale, pastel shades on the walls. Thin glasses, pure white china, and designer cutlery on the table. Gray recalled it had been an empty shell, another decaying wreck marring the Dickensian town. He hadn't even realised it had opened. Gray wondered how McGavin chose the place. It didn't seem his style.

These days it appeared as if half of Thanet, an officially deprived region with a high unemployment rate, a deluge of outsiders, increasing crime statistics, was attempting to pull itself up by its boot straps. The old, the tired, and the poor swept away to allow the fresh, the shiny, the cultured, to be catered for.

The London set with their barely occupied apartments of stainless steel and glass, here for the clean air, for a few days' rest and recuperation. Leaving those unable to keep up pushed away into the corners, steepening the downward spiral, widening the gap between the haves and the have-nots. Like tossing rubbish in the sea; the tide eventually dumped it elsewhere but by then it was out of sight and someone else's issue.

Gray had watched the changes happening with a question mark in his mind and doubt in his gut, often asking himself why people were so keen to see the past eliminated? And McGavin was getting in on the act.

"It's not an act," said McGavin, sat a table to the rear of the restaurant facing inwards so he could see everyone and everything. McGavin waved Gray to a seat opposite, where he would see nothing and no one besides McGavin. A waiter brought another seat for Hamson. "Are you sure you don't want anything to eat?"

"Yes," said Gray.

"On me."

"Definitely not," said Hamson.

"Too much like a bribe?" McGavin winked at Hamson.

"It'd stick in my throat, Frank," said Gray. "I'm not ready to die."

"Pity, our TripAdvisor ratings are pretty good, and rising. We'll soon be number one in the area."

"It's a surprise to see you as a restaurateur. Not your usual style."

"And what's my *usual style*, Sergeant Gray?"

"Drugs, prostitution, gambling..."

"That's slander. Everyone's got to eat." McGavin smiled. "Speaking of which, you don't mind if I carry on? Mediterranean fish stew, you know."

"Be my guest."

"I think it's you that's *my* guest." In between dipping a spoon into the bowl in the correct manner, sideways and pushing away from himself McGavin said, "How can I help you both?" He ruined the image of refinement by slurping.

"One of your employees, Larry Lost."

"Loser? He doesn't work for me. Not for quite a while. What's happened to him?"

"He's dead."

"Comes to us all, eventually," shrugged McGavin, no apparent impact on his appetite as he kept plunging the spoon. "How did he pass on?"

"Drowned." They were keeping the multiple stab wounds and crushed skull confidential for now.

"Nasty."

"We believe Larry was involved in the illegal transportation of immigrants from Europe," said Hamson.

"Really? I'm surprised. Alcohol and women were more his downfall."

"When did you last see him?"

Stew depleted, McGavin sat back and thought. He shook his head as, seemingly, his memory wouldn't play ball. "I don't know. A month? Maybe more? Our paths rarely crossed."

"I find that surprising. Thanet's a small place," said Gray. "And you two go back years."

"We do, you're right. Old mates; went to school together. It was me that gave him his nickname. Loser was useless at everything he did."

"Kind of you."

If McGavin detected the sarcasm in Gray's words he made no sign. He raised his hand to catch a waiter's eye. A young man trotted over.

"Yes, Mr McGavin?"

"Take this away." McGavin pointed at the bowl. "And keep a better watch on things, son. Be ready to look after clients rather than staring out the window at passers-by."

"Sorry, Mr McGavin. It won't happen again."

"You're right, it won't." McGavin flicked his fingers as if breezing away a fly. He returned his attention to Gray.

"Why did you two part ways?" asked Hamson.

"He'd been screwing up even more than usual, and I was moving into new lines of business which didn't really suit him."

"What new lines?" asked Hamson.

McGavin opened his arms to mean the restaurant. His expression showed he thought Hamson was stupid. "He came by a few times, kept asking for his job back until he stopped one day. I think he was pissed off at me. I heard he'd started working for someone else."

"Who?"

McGavin shrugged. "No idea. But they were welcome to him."

"You don't seem particularly cut up that an old mate, as you put it, is dead," said Gray.

"Is that a crime?"

"I suppose not. Just a little unusual."

"Well pardon me for not being as banal as you'd like."

"Have to hand it to you though, this place is nice."

"I'm rather proud."

"Do you own it?"

"Why is that anything to do with you, Sergeant?"

"Call it context."

McGavin smiled. "The property is leased, actually. The business rates are exorbitant. Crazy, given we're helping the struggling local economy."

"That's the trouble with tax."

The waiter interrupted them. He stood beside McGavin holding a plate.

"Are we done here?" said McGavin. "I've a rather fine hake fillet I'd hate to go cold."

Gray pushed back his chair, suddenly needing fresh air. Hamson rose too. "I'll come and find you if I've further questions."

"If you see the Maître D' on the way out I'm sure he'll get you a nice romantic table for an evening." McGavin smirked. "You make a good couple."

Outside, Gray leant on the railings and took in the sea view. Hamson stood beside him.

"What an arsehole," said Hamson.

"He's a man who's very convinced by himself."

"It seems like Jake has some competition between McGavin and Millstone."

"You know what, Von? It makes me wonder who really owns Millstone."

Hamson's phone rang. She answered, listened briefly, said a few words and disconnected. "That was Clough. The PM on Larry is about to start. I told him you'd head over."

Thirty Nine

Clough, in greens, was up to his arms inside Larry's chest cavity.

A microphone hung from the ceiling, near the pathologist's mouth. He would be speaking into it intermittently, recording his observations, though Gray couldn't hear as the speakers were switched off and there was a plate glass observation window between the theatre and waiting room.

The pathologist removed some organs from Larry, put them into the pan on a set of shiny scales, stepped back, and read the dial. The organs went into a dish beside Clough before he delved in once more.

The post mortem continued for nearly an hour. Part way through, just after Clough had used the bone saw (which Gray could hear, and it set his teeth on edge), he looked up and nodded at Gray briefly. When it was over, Clough exited the theatre via a set of double doors at the rear.

Eventually, after cleaning down and removing his scrubs, Clough joined Gray. "It's been a busy day," said the pathologist. "I put your boy here to the top of the queue. He didn't drown."

"No diatoms and plankton?"

"Well done. You remembered our lesson. Yes, diatoms and plankton only where they should be. Our Mr Lost had suffered extensive damage. Firstly, a fractured skull where he'd been hit by the hammer; not hard enough to kill but it would certainly have incapacitated him."

Gray remembered the small cabin. Perhaps Khoury didn't have the room to get a proper swing in?

Clough continued, "And then there were the knife wounds, eleven of them in all. A frenzied attack, I'd say. Loss of blood was acute. He'd have been in a lot of pain."

"So he didn't die quickly?"

"No, or easily."

"Have you had chance to look at William Noble?"

"The burning?" asked Clough. Gray nodded. "Briefly. It most likely wasn't the fire that killed him. The back of his head was smashed in too. I'll have to open him up to be sure, but I'd bet on not finding any smoke inhalation in the lungs."

Clough held out his hand, ready to make a wager.

"I'm not taking that," said Gray.

"Spoilsport."

GRAY WENT BACK TO HIS flat. After witnessing Larry being eviscerated he wanted some time by himself. While he cooked some pasta, he thought back to what McGavin had told him. Millstone appeared to be another common denominator, and he wondered what McGavin's connection was. When the pasta was done, he poured it into a bowl and carried it through to the living room. He sat at a table and booted up his laptop.

Having just bought and sold property, Gray broadly knew the ins and outs of the tortuous process; strictly speaking, his high-street solicitor had dealt with the detail. Gray had just been the cash machine. Perhaps commercial deals were different.

The police had access to the Land Registry where all details on property transfers since 1993 were held. Gray entered the restaurant's address and tapped the enter key.

His search revealed that only months ago it had indeed been purchased by Millstone Holdings. Prior to then it was owned by Enterprise Associated Partners. Gray moved over to a search engine. He entered "Millstone Holdings" and thumbed the enter key once more.

171,000 search results were returned. Gray scrolled through several pages. The few relevant links pointed to another official government body, Companies House, where trading information on commercial ventures was held. Like the Land Registry the police had full and free access to the data.

However, the information on Millstone Holdings was as deep as McGavin's stew. No trading history, no assets or liabilities, and the single director was someone called Fallon based at an address in Guernsey. Gray returned to the search engine and entered the address. Millstone wasn't the only business registered there. The search engine spewed out page after page of details. It appeared that Millstone was a shell company. Another search revealed Fallon was a London-based lawyer.

EAP was a different matter. There was over three decades of results. The business was wholly owned by Jake Armitage. Besides Jake, the other directors were his sons, Regan and Cameron.

Gray leaned back in his chair, not sure where to go next. Millstone seemed a dead end, its true ownership hidden away. Tomorrow he'd go to see the expert on property deals.

Jake.

Gray remembered his pasta. He skewered some with a fork and put it into his mouth. It was lukewarm but it would have to do. He switched his attention to the Sunset fire. The same search engine produced a raft of results. Gray flicked through the reports, not sure what he was looking for. He spotted an article by William Noble in the now-defunct *Thanet Echo*. It seemed like the newspaper still had a life in the virtual world. Gray clicked on it.

The article was written a few months after the blaze. It was the last edition put out by the Echo before it closed. The detail was a rehashing of the actual events followed by a summary of the following cases, including the injunction against the newspaper in a chronological order.

The guts of it was Noble's eyewitness account of the fire itself. It seemed he'd arrived on the scene with the fire engines and detailed what had occurred thereafter. Noble had had the foresight to grab his camera too. Right at the end, Noble stated that Jake's exoneration had resulted from someone admitting to setting the fire.

Larry Lost.

Apparently he'd thrown a cigarette end over the fence which had started the fire. An accident.

One photo embedded in the text had caught his eye. Gray scrolled back up until he found it. The image was of three people sitting side by side on the sea wall opposite the Sunset, their faces lit by the conflagration. Gray clicked so the photo was full screen. He recognised all three immediately.

Jeff Carslake was standing a few feet away from the couple who interested Gray most: Cameron Armitage with his arm around Rachel O'Shea.

Forty

In the morning, Gray's first port of call was the office of Tudor & Stratham, solicitors, who'd handled his house sale. They were based in what had been two large Victorian residences, now knocked through into one, located on the busy thoroughfare of Hawley Street in Margate near the law courts and the council offices. Gray pushed open the door and entered. Three people occupied four desks in the expansive reception area; only one looked up at Gray's appearance. Recognition lit up her face. The woman was called Annie Cartwright, Gray remembered.

"Oh, hello Mr Gray, we haven't seen you in a while."

"Not since I completed on the flat purchase, no. This time I'm here on police business." Now, the other two admin staff paid attention and took in Gray. Something more interesting than their paperwork.

"Of course. How can we help?" asked Annie.

"I've a question for Mister Stratham." He was the conveyancer who'd handled the process. An overly bright, horribly efficient man who clearly didn't have enough hours in the day to get everything on his to-do list done.

"I'll go fetch him." Cartwright moved out from behind her desk and climbed the nearby stairs. Within moments she was back. "Mister Stratham is free."

Stratham himself was halfway down the stairs, paused in the descent, obvious in his concern, feet on adjacent steps. He was a man keen to please, always ready with a smile which was big on width though small in depth. "Annie said there was a problem Mr Gray?"

"There's no problem, sir." Stratham blinked; Gray hadn't called him "sir" before. "I just want to benefit from your expertise."

"In that case, come on up!" Stratham flashed his trademark beam, turned around, and trotted up the remaining steps.

Gray followed, albeit at a more considered pace. He found Stratham in a large office at the front of the building, with a view of the street and a multi-storey car park through expansive bay windows. The space felt cramped, though. Paperwork and filing cabinets everywhere saw to that.

"Take a seat." Behind his desk, Stratham appeared comfortable and in control again after his earlier lack of equilibrium. "Can we get you a coffee?"

"No, thanks."

"So, how can I help?"

"I'm unable to go into details. I'm working on a case, and some information would possibly be useful."

"Exciting," said Stratham, leaning forward, elbows on the desktop, pupils glittering. "Ask away!"

"Some properties have changed hands recently, and I'd like to know a little more about them. Who owned them, who purchased them, and how much for."

"Which properties?"

Gray told Stratham, who wrote the addresses down, frowning. He said, "We may have handled these transactions."

"Is that a problem?"

"Probably not, all this sort of data is made publicly available anyway, though there may be some information I can't pass on. Client confidentiality and all that." Stratham grinned.

"I can always return with a warrant if we reach that point."

Stratham coughed. "No, no I'm sure that won't be necessary." Clearly Stratham was experiencing visions of uniformed police in his offices. "Can you give me a day or so to find out and get back to you?"

"That would be very helpful, thanks." Gray handed over his business card. "You can call me on that number. My email address is on there also."

Stratham showed Gray out. The only other time that had happened was when money changed hands, specifically from Gray to Stratham. The solicitor assured Gray he'd be able to help.

TWENTY MINUTES LATER, Gray was in another reception area, this time the headquarters of Jake's business, EAP, on Albion Street in Broadstairs. He was led through by an administrator to Jake's office, an understated affair with good views over the sea. Jake indicated for Gray to take a space on a tan and red leather sofa, a Chesterfield if Gray knew his furniture. Jake opted for the matching armchair. Between them was a low table, a tall and slender silver pot, matching milk jug, and two china mugs.

"You appreciate your coffee, if I remember correctly," said Jake.

"Yes."

"Unfortunately there aren't any roasters in Thanet, the nearest is in Canterbury. Ethiopian beans, supposedly from the very forest where coffee was first discovered."

Jake poured some for Gray. It was earthy and deep. But it was still coffee.

"I expected a bigger operation," said Gray. The building was a narrow five-floor terrace fronting the busy road right on the cliff top.

"I employ about fifty staff in all, across the pub and club. In this building we've got the finance and human resources departments, plus me. We don't need sales or marketing people, really, for what we do. The flats, the cleaners, even the caravan park, are dealt with through agencies."

"Everything you own is commercial property?"

"It's a roughly equal mix of commercial and residential. Mixing up the revenue streams across market segments minimises the risk."

"All under your company Enterprise Associated Partners?"

"Correct. Is that why you're here? To ask me about my business? Rather than to say you've found Regan's killer?"

"As soon as we've something to tell you we'll do so."

"It's taking too long."

"We're doing everything we can, Jake." Gray had another sip of the coffee, decided a change of tack was needed. "Who are the partners?"

Jake snorted. "There aren't any. The problem when you're starting out is you're small. Everything is tough: keeping your costs low because it's a volume market, getting a good price for what you sell and, even worse, gaining a credit rating. Cash – it's like blood for a company. If it isn't flowing right, you'll soon be out of business. So, one trick is to make yourself appear bigger than you are. It's all about front in the early days."

"What about now?"

"I'm established," shrugged Jake. "Roles are reversed. People come to me."

"Like Millstone?"

Gray noted Jake took a moment to think, gaining time by having some coffee. "As I said, people come to me all the time."

"What do you know about Millstone?"

"Only that they made me an offer I couldn't refuse."

"Who did you meet with? To arrange everything."

"Some lawyer called Fallon. Said he was Millstone's representative. He didn't even want to view the properties he bought, said that his people had already done their due diligence. He put an offer on the table, a very generous one, well above market rates, and I accepted. My solicitors handled the rest."

"You know who's in those properties now?"

"Of course. It's Frank McGavin. What do I care? I've no emotional attachment to what's basically bricks and mortar. You buy, you sell, make money along the way. That's all."

"It's just that I hear Millstone is everywhere now, trying to pick up property. Seems like you have a competitor. And they happen to be associated with the biggest criminal around here."

"So what? Competition comes and goes. McGavin simply leases the buildings, as far as I know. If he goes bust, it's his loss." Jake sighed, stood up, went to a cabinet in the corner of the room. He opened the doors, took out a bottle. He held it up to Gray. "Want one? It's malt, of course."

Gray would have expected nothing less. "On duty."

Jake poured himself a couple of fingers worth into a glass and brought it over. He drank half. "McGavin wanted to be a business partner." Jake stared into his glass for a moment – drained the whisky. "I refused to sell to him. It didn't feel right. Once you start with people like that you're never rid of them. Then Millstone came in and made an alternate, higher, bid. The timing was good, and it wasn't McGavin."

"Why sell now?"

"I've been thinking of retiring for some time. I've more money than I need, and I'm not enjoying it any more. I haven't for quite a while. Millstone has shown an interest in Seagram's as well. They made me an offer via Fallon. Not high enough, though. If they up it, I may just agree. Once I know what happened to Regan, and it's been dealt with I'll move out to my villa in Spain and never come back."

"How about Cameron? Couldn't he take over? He's a director of your business."

Jake laughed. "He's no bloody use. Too busy with his holier-than-thou pursuits."

"Like what?"

"I don't know. Some crap with the homeless. It doesn't matter, he's no entrepreneur anyway. The company would fold within a year if he got his hands on it. Better to sell, take the money, and stick it in the bank. At least the grandkids can have some of it, if that ever happens."

"He's still your son."

"He's nothing like me."

"Does that matter?"

"I don't know, Sol. Frankly, I'm not sure of anything anymore."

"On that point, there's been an accusation. About Regan."

"He's dead, who'd do that?"

"It has potential implications for the investigation."

"I'm assuming I won't like to hear this."

"There's a suggestion Regan used the fact he was your son to assault women."

"That's ridiculous," cut in Jake. Gray noted it was a half-hearted response.

"And that you covered it up by paying the women off."

Jake appeared ready to explode. His fingers gripped the arm of the chair. "My son is dead, and this is what you bring me?"

"We have to assess every potential line of enquiry."

"I think you need to go, Sol."

"Are you denying the accusation?"

"Get out."

Gray stared at Jake for a moment before leaving.

GRAY'S MOBILE RANG as he was stepping out onto Albion Street. It was the solicitor, Stratham.

"That was fast," said Gray.

"I ascertained that we didn't handle the sale and purchase of the two properties you mentioned."

"Is it a problem?"

"Not when I'm on the case, detective!" Stratham laughed. Gray didn't. "Erm, anyway, it only took a few calls, and it happens that a good friend of mine was the conveyancer. I managed to get the details out of him, provided there will be total confidentiality?"

"I'm a policeman, Mr Stratham. It goes with the territory."

"Of course, of course. Stupid of me. I've asked Annie to email you over the documents. They make interesting reading."

Gray wasn't so sure anything in the business of conveyancing could be classified as interesting, but he uttered positive noises before ringing off. By the time he opened up the app on his phone the email was there in his inbox. Stratham was nothing if not efficient. Gray found a bench round the corner, looking out to sea before he started reading.

Attached to the email were some fairly hefty documents – deeds, the search information, and a valuation document. The first wasn't a great deal of use. They were handwritten and dated back more than a century and not easy to read on a small screen. Useful as a historical document, was all.

The valuation document provided the proposed worth of the properties. Approaching half a million pounds for each. Not much more than Gray had paid for his flat. He called the solicitor again.

"Thanks for the information. Just one question. Do you think he got a good deal?"

"Yes, very. The price was about a hundred thousand pounds more than the current market figure. On both properties."

"Is that unusual?" asked Gray.

"The sale and purchase of a property is just a transaction, Sergeant Gray. What someone wants for it in terms of price and what someone else wishes to pay can be, and often are, completely disparate. This is where tension arises, of course. I'll ask you a question, what does a glass of tap water cost in a café or pub?"

"Nothing."

"So you wouldn't pay for it?"

"Why would I? It's freely available."

"And if you were in the middle of a desert, no water around you for miles and dying of thirst? What would you pay for that same glass of water now?"

"Probably everything I had."

"And that's exactly my point. Value depends upon context. It depends upon supply and demand. A glut of properties available means low prices, whereas a unique property in a desirable location means a high price. Take your new flat, for example. It's in a relatively exclusive arrangement, has a sea view in a popular area. You paid for that."

"I'm not so sure about exclusive," protested Gray.

"It's how the agent marketed it! And take the house you sold. Family-sized, within the catchment area for a raft of very good schools from reception through to Sixth Form. That's unique and desirable."

"I take your point."

Stratham, though, hadn't finished. "Sometimes an investor may take a gamble, picking up a property in a potentially underappreciated location in the hope it'll become popular and so drag the valuation up. Brick Lane in London, for example. A couple of decades ago it was full of squats and destitute artists. Now it's an expensive creative hub. Round here, Margate Old Town is the perfect example. Regenerated by the Turner Contemporary art gallery and on its way up. Clearly, Millstone think there's money to be made. Given how prices have moved around here recently, I think they're right. It won't be long before they recoup their investment. One hundred thousand pounds could seem like a snip."

"Thanks for the finance lesson, Mister Stratham."

"There's plenty more I can tell you!"

Gray hurriedly interjected. "That won't be necessary; you've given me enough to be going on with."

"My pleasure. The world of property management is a fascinating one. I wish there were more people like you who shared my enthusiasm! Come back if you need to know anything else."

Gray assured Stratham he would, then rang off. He rubbed his ear where it ached from the battering it had received from Stratham. His mobile rang again.

"Sergeant Gray? It's Rachel O'Shea. I must speak with you about William Noble's murder. I can tell you who killed him."

"Where are you?"

"At the Lighthouse. Please come as soon as you can." She disconnected.

Gray called Hamson, told her what little he knew, and agreed to meet her outside the Lighthouse as soon as he could get there.

Forty One

"What the hell is going on, Sol?" asked Hamson as soon as she got out of her car. She'd parked on double yellows right out the front, the same as Gray. Before Gray could answer, the front door to the Lighthouse opened. Natalie beckoned them, turned, and went inside.

"I guess we'll learn in a minute," said Gray.

They found Natalie in the refectory, standing beside one of the long tables. Rachel was already seated and looking uncomfortable. It couldn't be easy perching on the hard surface while heavily pregnant. Natalie sat down too, pointing at the space opposite.

"Sergeant Gray said you wanted to tell us about the circumstances of William Noble's death," said Hamson as she settled.

"William Noble was killed for what he knows about Millstone," said Natalie. "They're at the centre of everything."

"Why don't you start at the beginning," said Gray.

Natalie straightened her back, keeping her forearms on the table. She said, "This is where Rachel should speak."

Gray and Hamson switched their attention to the younger woman. However, Rachel was staring at Natalie, who put her hand on Rachel's arm. "It's time," said Natalie.

"Over a decade now since they died," said Rachel. "It seems like yesterday."

"Who?" asked Hamson. But Gray knew. He was hearing echoes of his own past.

"My family."

"The beginning, Rachel, as Sergeant Gray asked," said Natalie gently.

Rachel gathered herself, took in a deep breath, let it out. "We used to live in Hackney. Me, my younger brother, mother, and father. Jonathan, Felicity, and Dean they were called. We weren't allowed to call her Mum, just Felicity. Dean was just, well, Dad. Rachel glanced at Natalie who lowered her eyes and stared at the table top.

"I remember being happy, until my parents split up. Felicity said that Dad was holding her back, that she needed space as an artist. The three of us moved out, leaving Dad behind. After that, it was a carefree existence shifting from house to house. Sometimes staying for a day, or a week, or a month. For us kids it was fun at first. Felicity made it into a game. Finding food, staying up as late as we wanted, meeting other interesting, sometimes crazy people. Living, she called it.

"But it wasn't long before the experience became a lot less enjoyable. My mother, she was flaky. It was Dad who'd kept her together, and once he was gone … She hid it well at first, and we were too young to know any better. Until the money ran out, and the paranoia crept in."

"Felicity began saying she was a free spirit, as if she was some '60s hippy. She'd dress up too, wearing outrageous clothes, altering her hair. It was like she was trying to be someone else. We kids were a drag."

Natalie stood up and went to look out of the window.

"Until one day she just upped and disappeared, leaving behind most of her stuff. My brother and I woke up one morning in a bedsit, and we were alone. She'd left a note saying she loved us, but we were better off without her."

"How old were you?"

"I was thirteen, Jonathan was nine."

"You must have had to grow up quickly," said Gray.

Rachel emitted a sharp, humourless laugh. "You have no idea. School? We never went near the place. Mum had claimed we were home tutored when anyone bothered to ask."

"What happened when your mother went missing?"

"I took Jonathan to the nearest police station. At least we got a hot drink and some food there. We were put into care for nearly a week. Jonathan and I were split up. It took them that long to find my dad. When he turned up to collect me, it was the best day ever. He gave me a huge hug. He was crying. Said he'd been searching for us for ages. Then we went home."

Gray felt a sharp pang of envy. A father reunited with a lost child. It was everything he had wanted for the last ten years. Out of the corner of his eye he saw Hamson glance over at him.

"That must have been an amazing feeling," said Gray.

Rachel smiled briefly. "It was, for a few years. We went to school, made friends, had some stability. Dad was a taxi driver, did all hours just to make ends meet. We had a happy life, heard nothing from Mum. One day Dad told us we were going on holiday. To Margate, every Londoner's dream. We were so excited.

"He booked a B&B not far from here. Sunset, it was called, small, clean, and near the beach. We had a room on the top floor, up some narrow stairs. Only a handful of residents. And it was run by a lovely old lady, Mrs Renishaw. Just a few days to get away, that's all." Rachel paused, staring down at the cuticles on her left hand, her eyes seemingly focused on them.

"It was the last night of the holiday; I'd spent so much time awake looking out for Jonathan while we were with Felicity that I was used to getting by on only a few hours, still am. My dad tried to stop me leaving, but I got past him and ran out the front door, down the narrow stairs. There was nobody around. The sea, it drew me. I sat on the harbour arm for an age, just listening to the beat of the tide. It was mesmerising. Until the sirens. Fire engines and police cars racing along the road and up the hill.

"I had a terrible feeling in the pit of my stomach. I can remember it still. A wrenching and twisting as if there was a big hand inside me, squeezing." Rachel paused for a moment – zoned out and in the past – until she shook her head and came back. "I forgot the waves and followed the light. There was an orange glow over the town, as if the sun was rising even though it was the middle of the night.

"When I got back to the B&B, fire engines were spraying water on the blaze. The flames were leaping out the windows. Mrs Renishaw was crying. I ran through the small crowd of on-lookers, looking for Dad and Jonathan."

Rachel fell silent, her hands at rest.

"When the fire was out, they found them in the bedroom. The fire caught quickly. I learned later it was because Mr Renishaw, the old man who owned the guest house, had flammable materials lying around. They gave off toxic fumes. I blamed myself for years."

"Why?" asked Gray.

"I should have been there. If I'd have stayed, maybe I'd have been able to raise the alarm."

"You don't know that," said Natalie. "I've told you a thousand times."

"And afterwards?" asked Hamson.

"I was in care again until Dad's sister, my aunt, took responsibility for me. I went back to school, worked hard, and got good grades. What else was there to do? Then to University to do a teaching degree. Rather than working in London, I applied for a job here in a small school, and I got it. It felt right to be in Margate, because I'd never really left. How could I?

"Then my life took another unexpected turn. Some people came in to speak with the children. They were from a charity called the Lighthouse Project. In walked Felicity." Rachel turned to Natalie and touched her hand. "My mother."

Gray struggled to make sense of what she'd just said. Natalie was the mother from hell? The one who'd abandoned her kids. The same as he effectively had.

"How could you?" he asked. Then Gray wondered what his daughter might say about him.

"I take after my father," said Rachel. "It was Jonathan who was like Mum."

"What happened to Felicity?" asked Gray.

Natalie shook her head. "She's gone, I made sure of it."

"What happened when you met again?" asked Gray.

"I couldn't believe it," said Rachel. "She'd been missing from my life for so long, and then she was there. By pure chance. It didn't matter what wigs she wore, what make-up she had on; I always recognised my mother. And I didn't think she recognised me. I couldn't stay; I kept my head down, turned around, and walked out."

"And I ran after her," said Natalie. "I tried to tell her everything, but she didn't want to know."

"Can you blame me?"

Gray heard the anger in Rachel's tone and saw her shoulders tense.

Natalie reached out and took Rachel's hands in her own. "Of course not."

Rachel visibly relaxed. "It took months of persistence on my mum's part before I could bring myself to see her again. When we did finally meet, I was glad."

"Catching up on all the lost time?" asked Hamson.

"Not at first," said Natalie. "Before seeing Rachel at the school I'd no idea she'd come back to Margate. Maybe part of me hoped she had. If I'd known for sure I'd have tried sooner. I had to explain to Rachel who actually killed our family. Even if it meant she never spoke to me again it was imperative I tell her it was because of that bastard, Jake Armitage."

The silence was utter; the accusation swinging in the air like a body on the end of a hangman's rope. Twisting, turning, demanding attention.

"That's a very serious allegation," said Hamson. "Do you have anything to back it up?"

Natalie stood up and left the room briefly. Within a minute she returned, dropped a folder onto the table. She sat back down, opened the folder, and pushed it over to Gray and Hamson. She said, "William gave me these. It was another of his projects. One which got stopped."

Gray spread out the contents which were mainly neatly cut newspaper clippings, from a variety of sources. The locals were prevalent – the *Thanet Echo* and the *Kent Herald*. Each was cut so the date at the top was visible and ordered in a chronological review of the fire and its aftermath. The bodies discovered, the speculation that it was for financial gain, the denial from Jake, the lack of evidence which meant it never got taken any further, a case dropped by the CPS much to local outrage, the subsequent development of the dilapidated site from which Jake apparently profited. Gray noticed the article written by Noble that he'd read last night wasn't present.

"Why didn't Noble go to the police?"

"He tried, but your lot wouldn't touch it."

Hamson frowned. "We would have at least looked at it."

"You point-blank refused. Told William to take a hike or he'd be arrested for wasting police time."

"Do you know who told him that?" asked Gray.

"Jeff Carslake."

Forty Two

Hamson was nursing a coffee at a table in the corner of the staff canteen where it was slightly less noisy. A cup of coffee and a bacon roll awaited Gray at the adjacent space. He sat and put Natalie's folder between them. He reached out for the roll and took a bite.

"Did you believe any of that bullshit from those two?" asked Gray, the food sticking in his throat. "How could Rachel possibly forgive Natalie so easily? She walks out, leaves her kids, the whole family dies, and suddenly it's okay?"

"Natalie is the only relative Rachel has left, and she's pregnant. Wouldn't you want your mother at a time like that?"

"And Natalie isn't even her real name. What else has she been lying about? I'm going to have another talk with Rachel on her own. She mentioned Felicity or Natalie, or whatever her name, was wearing wigs."

"Frankly Sol, I'm more focused on our boss, your friend, possibly being involved in covering up — or even committing — a crime." Hamson reached over for the folder, opened it, and flipped through the articles.

"That's probably a lie too."

"What do you remember about the Sunset fire?"

"Not much, I wasn't in the best of places at the time. Jake vigorously denied the accusations. He went so far as to take out an injunction against both *The Echo* and *The Herald*. *The Echo*, where Noble was the editor, went into administration as a result. It didn't do Noble's career much good. He never forgot it. Everything was different. Carslake was a sergeant, McGavin was just a bit-part player in those days. The big dog was Duncan Usher, he ran everything."

"Where's Usher now? Died in a fire by any chance?"

"He's in prison for murder."

Hamson closed the folder and looked at Gray. "When you met Noble he said nothing about all of this?"

"No, it was all focused on Millstone."

"You're sure?"

"Bloody hell, Von, yes. I'm sure." Gray held back mentioning Noble's story. Hamson would be all over it, focusing on Carslake instead of the case at hand.

"Obviously we need to check into Natalie's claim that Noble brought this in, and we ignored it."

"Agreed."

"Who else would have been here at the time?"

"Fowler. He was a DC back then."

"Mike can't have been involved." Hamson dismissed the possibility with a wave of her hand. "Carslake, though ..."

"I was there Von, I heard it too. I can't get my head around everything."

"I knew something wasn't right with him."

"Von, I've got to say I think you're seeing something which isn't here. You and Carslake have never got on. You can't be judge, jury, and executioner here. It's one woman's word against a career copper. A woman, I add, who we know for sure lies."

"There's something Sol, I'm sure of it. We need to talk to Carslake."

"I doubt Carslake will take kindly to hearing this from me, never mind you."

"We can't leave this."

"I'm due to go out with him tonight. Mike will be with us too."

Hamson blinked. "Mike's going?"

"Didn't he tell you?"

"No."

"He mentioned going out for a beer some time so I took him up on the offer."

Hamson stood up. "We're not married. He can do what he wants. And you have to go, Sol." She leaned over Gray. "Talk to Carslake."

Gray suddenly felt his stomach churn again and a burn in his throat. "Sure, whatever." He walked quickly to the toilets, leaving a puzzled Hamson behind. Inside a stall he threw up, the coffee and roll he'd just consumed splashing against the bowl. He retched twice more. He felt drained, literally.

At the sinks, Gray swilled water around his mouth and spat. He washed his face. He saw his reflection in the mirror. His face looked thin. All this bloody treachery was taking its toll.

Forty Three

Gray glanced around the office. Nobody was paying him the slightest attention. He called up the HOLMES2 database, typed in "Sunset, fire". He clicked through the reports and interviews. Carslake had been involved in many of them. A coroner's investigation recorded accidental death.

Mr Renishaw, it seemed, liked to tinker with motorbikes. The belief was he'd left flammable materials lying around in the garden and kitchen which had caught fire when someone threw a cigarette stub over the fence.

The data Gray reviewed appeared perfectly reasonable. Evidence and conclusion neatly followed each other. Gray sat back, starting to feel perhaps Hamson's suspicions were correct, though there was only Natalie's word that Noble had been in. A hand slapped him on the shoulder.

"Bloody hell, Sol, you look like you've seen a ghost!" said Fowler.

"You startled me, Mike."

"Just wanted to check we were still on for tonight."

"Nothing's changed."

"Good, see you later."

Gray made sure Fowler was at his desk before he accessed the shared folder where all the information on the Regan Armitage case was stored. He quickly found Fowler's CCTV footage. There was one marked "Seagram's" and dated the night Regan had gone missing.

He slowly worked his way through the footage, reviewing the external scenes first, then the internal ones. Fowler had been right: other than the time when the couple departed there was no clear image of the woman in the blue wig. When she appeared in the footage she kept her face away from the camera, like she knew it was watching.

Finally, Gray carried out a database search of reported assaults in connection with Seagram's or Regan. There was nothing, not a single piece of documented evidence. So either Quigley was lying or Regan was simply a player.

Forty Four

Then

The interview room smelt of cigarette smoke. From a previous occupant, not William Noble. He held a plastic cup of something lukewarm from the vending machine. From the doorway Carslake watched Noble swirl the liquid around.

Carslake wanted to leave the door open, to draw some fresher air in from the corridor, but he couldn't. He didn't want stray ears overhearing this conversation. The catch clicked shut. Noble half rose from his seat. Carslake waved him back down.

"Good to see you, Sergeant," said Noble.

Carslake merely grunted in reply. Having the editor of the local newspaper turn up on your doorstep was never a positive sign. He had a nose for things, did Noble.

"You asked to see me," said Carslake. He remained standing, making it clear that the discussion would be brief.

"I know you've been involved in the investigation into the Sunset fire, the guest house, right?"

"What of it?"

"I think it was deliberate."

"Arson, you mean?"

"Yes."

"That's not what the official report says," replied Carslake.

"I believe differently."

"I didn't know you were an expert on fires and their cause."

"I'm not."

"Then why are we having this conversation? Conclusions were drawn, the investigation is closed."

"It's Jake Armitage. He profited from the fire."

Carslake let gravity take hold, and he sat down. This needed handling. "It's well known Mister Armitage owned the building. It's also well known the land has since been developed."

"Yes, but did you know that until the fire, the Renishaws were refusing to sell to him? The whole redevelopment hinged on the guest house. If it fell through, everything did."

"So?"

"So the deal was twenty-four hours away from collapsing. Don't you think it's remarkable the Sunset then burns down, salvaging the whole thing?"

"The only aspect which sounds remarkable is your claim, Will. What proof do you have?"

"I've spoken to the owner's daughter. She told me all about the offer from Jake. Threats and harassment too, apparently, after it was rejected."

"Again, do you have any proof?"

"Isn't the daughter's word enough?"

"No. Do you have anything else?"

"Not yet. I thought you'd be interested. Isn't this what the police are supposed to do? Investigate?"

Carslake got to his feet and leaned on the table, knuckles on the scratched formica, towering over Noble. "I don't hear anything worthy of my time, frankly. Now, if you have something solid, I'll happily investigate. Until then I'd suggest you stop spreading malicious rumours about Mr Armitage, otherwise you and I could be having a very different conversation."

Noble blinked at Carslake. His mouth flapped open a couple of times but no words came out. Carslake opened the door and stood by it for a few moments until Noble got up and wandered out.

"This isn't the last you'll hear of this," said Noble as he passed by.

Carslake grabbed Noble's upper arm and squeezed. "You want to be arrested for wasting police time, Will? Be my guest."

Noble shook Carslake off and left.

Outside, Carslake took out his mobile phone, called Jake, and told him what had happened.

"Is it true?" asked Carslake.

"That's not your concern, Jeff. Your job is to keep people like Noble at bay. I'll keep a closer eye on him from now on."

Jake rang off, leaving Carslake in the dark.

Forty Five

Now At the halfway stage of the quiz, during a break to allow the participants to stock up on beer, Gray raised the matter. It was noisy, the chatter of a full pub talking about the questions so far. Nobody would overhear. Gray's team was lying in fourth place, just a handful of points off the lead.

When Fowler returned with three pints Gray said, "Do either of you remember the fire which burned down the Sunset guest house?"

Fowler chugged his lager then nodded. "Sure. I wasn't on duty that night, but I remember."

"Why?" asked Carslake.

"There's been an accusation that Jake was involved in burning down Noble's office."

"Based on what?"

"A claim that Noble made a connection between Jake and the Sunset fire ten years ago, and it got swept under the carpet. We were all working here at the time, but I was on leave."

"What are you suggesting?" asked Fowler.

"Nothing, I just wanted to know if either of you knew of Noble making these claims?"

"Means nothing to me," said Fowler.

"Apparently it's related to Millstone Developments."

Carslake gave Gray a tiny shake of the head which Fowler didn't see.

"Who?" asked Fowler.

"They're property developers."

Carslake frowned. However, the quiz master chose that moment to pick up the microphone. His voice boomed through the loudspeakers. "All right, ladies and gentlemen, are you ready for the rest of the questions?" There was a resounding "yes!" from the tables, except Gray's. "Then let's get going! Question twenty-six ..."

FORTY MINUTES LATER and Fowler was totting up their results. "Bloody hell, what happened to us in the second half? We got hardly any right!"

"My fault," said Gray. "I couldn't think straight."

"We'll do better next time," said Carslake.

"Want another?" Fowler raised his empty glass.

"I'm done," said Gray.

"Me too," said Carslake.

"Looks like I'm on my own, then. See you tomorrow." Fowler went to the bar.

Gray followed Carslake out to his car. Carslake unlocked, got inside. Gray got in the passenger side.

"Why on earth did you bring up Noble and Millstone?" asked Carslake.

"Hamson and I spoke to Natalie Peace and Rachel O'Shea. Turns out they're mother and daughter. Millstone is trying to buy the property their charity is located in. Noble was investigating Millstone. They're convinced Noble was murdered to silence him. They're also convinced Jake had a hand in the Sunset fire which killed their family. That's why I brought it up."

"Their family?"

"Natalie's ex-husband and son died. Rachel was there at the time but happened to be outside when the fire started."

"Horrible business."

"You do remember it then?"

"Yes. Unfortunately. The sort of thing you'd like to forget."

Gray waited for more; he didn't get it. "You were there during the fire?"

"I was on duty, it was near the station. It shouldn't come as a surprise."

"Why did you stop me asking about Noble?"

"Do you trust me?"

Gray hesitated before he answered. "Of course I do."

"Good." If Carslake had noticed Gray's hesitation, he made nothing of it. "This has to stay between us, okay?"

"Promise. Cross my heart."

"First, I don't know anything about Noble coming into the station about Jake. I seriously doubt he ever did. Noble was always seeing a story where there wasn't one. Plus, later on, he had a vendetta against Jake. The Sunset fire brought down Noble's newspaper, and he always tried to return the favour."

"I know."

"Second, Millstone is a sensitive subject. We think it's being used as a vehicle to buy up large swathes of Margate. There's a high-level investigation underway, very sensitive, very quiet. There may be some issues with local departments like planning. Bungs – stuff like that. Even I don't know a great deal about it."

"Jake's the victim here?"

"They seem to be targeting him specifically, though he is the largest property owner in Thanet."

"Jake mentioned that he'd been thinking of retiring and that he'd been made an offer on Seagram's."

"It's entirely possible. Who could blame him for moving on? Look, we need to work together on this."

"How?"

"You've gained the women's trust, right?"

"I wouldn't go that far."

"You know them, though. I don't."

"Yes."

"Then you need to keep them off Millstone and Jake for now."

"I'm not sure I can. They're pretty driven."

"You have to. I don't want them buggering up the investigation."

"Why?"

"They're biased. Their charity is under threat from Millstone, and they hold a grudge against Jake. That's enough, isn't it?"

"I'll try."

"And Hamson; she can't know about the Millstone investigation either. Too sensitive."

"I don't like the sound of that, Jeff."

"That's how it has to be."

Gray thought for a few moments, weighing everything up. He wasn't sure where Carslake was going with this, but it felt best to be on the inside. "Okay."

Carslake held out his hand. "It's great spending time with you again, Sol. I've really missed it."

Gray shook. Carslake grinned. Gray forced himself to do the same.

"See you tomorrow," said Gray. He got out of the car and began to walk home through Broadstairs, plenty on his mind.

On the way, he sent Hamson a text.

Forty Six

Hamson arrived at Gray's flat five minutes after he did. He buzzed her in, left the front door ajar, and went to stand on the balcony. He listened to the beat of the waves until Hamson was beside him.

"Want a coffee?" said Gray.

"Got anything stronger?"

"Just beer."

"Coffee it is then."

Gray left Hamson on the balcony while he made the drinks. He carried two mugs out, passed one over.

"How did it go?" she asked.

"Mike doesn't know anything, and Carslake had a different perspective on the situation."

Hamson snorted. "Well, he would. What bullshit did he feed you this time?"

"He didn't recall Noble coming into the station, and I couldn't find any record of him doing so either."

"That doesn't mean anything. Documents can be amended. Or not filed."

"Carslake repeated that Noble loathed Jake too. Meaning he was biased against him."

"Is that it?"

"Carslake also mentioned an investigation into Millstone and said I needed to trust him, that there were larger events going on behind the scenes."

This time Hamson outright laughed. "Yes, like saving his career. God, the man has you twisted around his little finger!"

Gray had been about to give Hamson all the detail on the Millstone investigation but decided now to keep it to himself. She'd developed her own bias and because of that he felt he couldn't trust her.

"Are you saying I'm compromised, Sol?" Hamson banged the coffee cup down on the table.

"Yes."

"That makes two of us, then. You're too close to Carslake and Jake. You can't see what's actually going on around you." Gray didn't appreciate the accusation; it went against everything he'd stood for in his police career. He bit down, felt his jaw muscles flex with the effort, counted to ten.

"I see very clearly."

"Really? How much are you affected by your friendship with Carslake? What about that he's helping you find Tom?"

"Irrelevant."

"Is it? Has Carslake organised it so you can see this so-called witness yet?"

"No, but to be fair there hasn't been a lot of chance."

"Fair? What's fair got to do with it? This is your son we're talking about, and Carslake is dithering. Stop defending the indefensible and wake up, Sol!"

"Where's the evidence?"

"God, listen to yourself!"

"We're police, Yvonne; this is one of our own."

"And what if I tell you I intend bringing in Jake tomorrow morning for the Sunset fire?"

"I'd say we don't have the evidence to arrest him."

"Jake will be helping with our investigation. Think of it as shaking the tree and watching what falls out."

"Out of a job if you're not careful, Von."

"People *died*, Sol. It's important they have justice."

"This is wrong."

"No, *you're* wrong!"

"We'll see about that."

Hamson turned and left the flat. Gray knew he should go after her; reassure her that he was on her side. But he couldn't bring himself to. He wasn't certain of much right now. All he knew for sure was that his stomach was churning, and he felt sick yet again.

Forty Seven

When Gray got into the station the following morning, he headed for the canteen and grabbed a coffee. Yet again he couldn't stomach any food. He'd had to notch his belt tighter today. His clothes were beginning to hang off him. Standing waiting to pay, he felt a nudge in his back.

"At last," said Fowler. "Glad you've made it in."

"What's going on?"

"Yvonne brought Jake Armitage in last night. She's questioning him now. The station is abuzz, haven't you noticed?"

Gray hadn't. Though – now Fowler mentioned it – there was an urgency and excitement in the canteen. Lots of smiles and laughter. He'd been too focused upon himself. "For what?"

"The Sunset fire."

She'd done it then. "We should be focusing on trying to find Khoury, not this."

"No argument from me, Sol."

"How did Carslake react?"

Fowler shrugged. "I haven't seen him yet. Here's Yvonne, though."

Hamson entered and made her way directly over to Gray. "A word," she said. Fowler raised an eyebrow at Gray as Hamson spun away. Gray could read Hamson's emotion like a book printed in an oversized font. Defiance was written all over her face.

"I hear Jake's in custody," said Gray.

"I had him brought in last night. We've just taken a break."

"Are you getting anywhere?"

"No, he won't answer any questions. He wants to speak with you."

"Why?"

"He won't say."

A fact which was clearly niggling Hamson. Gray asked, "What room's he in?"

Hamson didn't answer immediately, just stared at Gray. "You're too close to all of this, Jake. The case. You two are like best buddies."

"Yeah, you said last night."

"Carslake told me. All about Millstone, the investigation. Why didn't you?"

"Honestly? I was about to until you went off on one again. And Carslake ordered me not to."

"I'm your commanding officer. Don't you trust me?"

"Of course, but Carslake's both our commanding officers. What he says goes. That's the chain, Von."

Hamson leant forward, got right into Gray's line of sight. "I know what you're up to."

"What are you talking about?" Gray was genuinely perplexed. He'd never seen Hamson like this.

"With Carslake. Trying to get shot of me. All for a promotion. I thought you of all people were beyond stepping on others to move up."

"I'm not interested in your job."

"That's not what I hear."

"From who?"

"The who doesn't matter, it's the why."

"How many years have we worked together?"

"Almost four."

"And in that time when have I ever done anything to undermine you?"

"Times and people change."

"Someone's lying to you."

Hamson nodded. "You're absolutely right, Sergeant Gray. The culprit is looking right at me."

"Von, this is ridiculous. Listen to yourself. You're paranoid." As soon as he said it, Gray groaned inside. He'd gone too far.

Hamson stood up and leaned over him. "From now on, it's Guv, Boss, or Ma'am. No more friendly first-name stuff. Get it?"

Gray nodded. "In spades."

"About time you did. He's in three." Hamson walked out, leaving the wreckage of a friendship in her wake.

Forty Eight

Jake wasn't alone. The lawyer, Neil Wright, sat beside him.

"I'll leave you two on your own," said Wright, offering his chair to Gray. "Remember my advice, Jake."

"You don't look happy, Sol," said Jake as Wright closed the door. Jake was dishevelled, untidy, his hair a mess. As if he'd been up most of the night. "Is our history causing you some trouble with Inspector Hamson?"

"You wanted to speak to me."

"Yes, I thought I owed it to you."

"You don't owe me anything."

"For old time's sake."

"That's irrelevant now."

"When the interview restarts I'll be confessing to the Sunset fire. I ordered the place burned down. The deaths of that family are on me."

"Why now?"

"Regan's passing has made me think a great deal."

"I don't believe you."

Jake leaned forward. "And that's why I wanted to talk before Hamson gets her claws in. This is necessary. There are bigger things going on here than just me."

"Like what?"

"I'm asking you to drop your investigation into Regan's death."

"Why that the sudden change of heart?"

"Because we used to be friends."

"What's McGavin's connection to all of this? He must be involved somehow if Wright is representing you."

"It doesn't matter. Everything's in motion now. You can't stop it, Sol. That's what I'm telling you. Let events take their course."

"No."

"Family's important. I've never really been there for my kids, particularly not for Cameron. I spent all my time looking out for Regan. Well now it's time to fix that. I'm going to be a grandfather. This is my chance to make it all right. I've signed my business over to Cameron, so he can provide for the child and Rachel."

"Rachel O'Shea?"

"They've been an item for a while. I'm pleading with you to give Cameron a chance. I'm taking the fall for everything." Jake held out a hand for Gray to shake. "Please, Sol. One last deal for me."

Gray suddenly felt hot. "I'll tell your lawyer to come back in."

Jake let his hand fall, and Gray left. He went into the toilets and washed his face with cold water. It barely helped. He threw up into the sink, retching until there was no more in his stomach.

He looked at himself in the mirror. Pale, haggard, bloodshot eyes.

"You look like shit, Sol." It was Fowler, standing in the doorway.

"Upset stomach."

"That's not what me and Von reckon. It's not the first time you've been sick, is it?"

"I'm all right."

"You're not, Sol. I've known you for years. You're a stubborn bastard. I'm telling you, get to a doctor."

Gray knew Fowler was right. "I will. Soon."

"Good. Meanwhile, we've got a body. You'll want to see who it is."

Forty Nine

"I can think of worse places to die," said Fowler.

"There are plenty better, though," replied Gray. He was standing above Khoury's corpse, his eyes wide open, mouth clamped shut, as if he'd been straining at the moment something in his body snapped. Khoury was facing the sea, slumped at the rear of the old casino on the Ramsgate main bay. Once a grand building with plenty of money flowing through the doors, it now stood abandoned. Another relic of times past.

The immediate area was popular with winos and derelicts, indicated by the sand strewn with rubbish: bottles, cans, cigarette ends, and the odd syringe. The beach area had been cordoned off down to the water, as far as the harbour wall one way, and a couple of hundred yards to the other, towards the mothballed beach fairground. Uniform were combing the area picking up every item and putting it into a bag in case it proved to be evidence.

Graffiti was daubed on the wall, and the air reeked of urine and stale alcohol. There were, however, none of the local colourful characters in sight.

Gray squatted down for a closer look at Khoury's left arm. It was bound by a tourniquet, and a needle was shoved in one vein, the plunger fully depressed. By Khoury's right hand was the remaining drug paraphernalia – lighter, foil, and wrap of narcotics.

"Overdose," said Fowler unnecessarily.

"Convenient."

"Who cares?"

I do, thought Gray but kept his opinion to himself. His phone buzzed, and he pulled it out; it was a text from the solicitor, Stratham. Gray read it and realised loose ends were being tied up. For him too.

He rang the Lighthouse. Kelvin answered.

"Is Rachel there?" asked Gray.

"Sure, I'll get her."

"Hello?" said Rachel.

"It's DS Gray, can we talk?"

"I was hoping you'd ask."

"WHAT IS IT SUPPOSED to mean?" whispered Rachel.

"I haven't a clue," Gray replied.

The Turner Contemporary was a modern art gallery a few hundred yards down the hill from the station and a short drive from the Lighthouse. The exhibit in question was a lacquered branch lying on a mattress. The artist was local-girl-done-good, Tracey Emin.

But they weren't here for the art. Gray led Rachel into a darkened room with several rows of benches. There was a film on a loop playing against one wall. At this time of day, the gallery was almost empty. At the front was a couple, wearing headphones to hear the commentary, but there was nobody else in earshot.

Gray and Rachel sat as far away from the pair as possible and kept their voices low.

"Thanks for agreeing to meet me here," Rachel said.

"No trouble."

"Did you find any record of Noble meeting with Carslake?"

"No," admitted Gray. "You should know that Adnan Khoury, has been found dead."

Rachel put a hand to her mouth. "How?"

"We're yet to confirm for sure but it seems he took an overdose."

"Oh my God, that's awful. Poor man."

"I'm struggling to understand your relationship with your mother."

"What do you mean?"

"After what happened, what she did, you somehow seem to be close. It must have been hard."

Rachel paused for a moment. The film had ended, and the couple moved outside, leaving Gray and Rachel alone. She appeared to sag. "I hate her for what she did, but she's the only family I have left. I'm trying to make it work. Of course it's not easy. She's not easy."

"In what way?"

"It's difficult to explain. I guess I'm never sure if she's telling the truth or spinning me a line. The thing is, Sergeant Gray, I've been alone for a long time. At first, once I'd got over the anger, I was just over the moon at having my mother back. She couldn't replace Dad or Jonathan, but it had to be better than nobody, right?"

"Yes." Gray understood exactly what Rachel meant. "What about Cameron? Jake told me earlier he's the father."

Rachel rubbed her belly again. She smiled. "We met when we were kids."

"I know; I saw a photo of you two, outside the Sunset that night."

"It was stupid really, trying to reclaim a lost love. How could it work after everything we've both been through?"

"So you're not together now?"

"No. We tried, and this little miracle I'm carrying is because of those efforts, but we split up after a couple of months. There's too much baggage between us, too much time. If the fire hadn't happened, who knows?"

"What was Cameron and Regan's relationship like?"

"Regan wanted to be Cam's big brother, but Cam couldn't even stand being in the same room as him. He loathed Regan."

"Why?"

"He's never said, but I think it was to do with me. It was something else that came between us. His constant anger about the past."

"Talking about the past, when we spoke the other day you said your mother used to wear wigs?"

"Yes."

"What about now?"

"No, she sticks with the same old hair colour now. Although, I did see one in her flat recently. I was surprised to be honest."

"What colour was it?"

"Blue."

Gray grabbed Rachel's arm. "Was Natalie at the Lighthouse when you left?"

"Yes, why? What's the matter?"

But Gray didn't answer. Walking quickly, he left Rachel in the projection room and pulled out his mobile.

"Where did you get to?" asked Fowler, sounding annoyed. "You just cleared off."

"Not now, Mike! I need you to get over to the Lighthouse and bring Natalie Peace in for questioning. Now."

"On what charge?"

"The murder of Regan Armitage."

Fifty

Cameron Armitage was at the mobile home site, in the bar, wiping down the tables. He didn't acknowledge Gray's entrance.

"I guess you won't be doing this for much longer," said Gray. "Now you've sold EAP to Millstone. How much were you offered?"

Cameron didn't pause in his task. "That's private business."

"Was this the plan all along? Get your father out of the way, then sell his assets? As the sole director of the business now, you have the right to do so. Your father incapacitated and Regan dead."

"EAP had financial difficulties already and Jake being charged has panicked our suppliers and partners. I decided it was worth taking the cash now, while we still can."

"This is just a sideshow though, isn't it, Cameron? The money's simply a bonus. Really, this is about payback."

"You don't know what you're talking about, Sergeant."

"You hated Regan because he took something from you – Rachel. The fire he set at the Sunset all those years ago drove you two apart. You tried to get back together again, but it didn't work. Because of Regan. So you wanted revenge. And you had the perfect partners to help pull it off: McGavin wanted EAP, and Natalie wanted Jake to suffer. Your father was caught in a pincer movement between you two.

"Regan was a player. I bet he thought the idea of sleeping with your ex-girlfriend's mother would grate on you. But what he didn't realise, was that he was the one being played. Some ketamine went into his drink, and he was bundled out of the club, insensible. Then he was loaded into a vehicle and taken to Ramsgate harbour, put aboard Larry Lost's boat, and dumped at sea, making it look like he was running migrants on the side and drowned in the process. How am I doing?"

"Very inventive. Where's your proof?"

"We've plenty of circumstantial evidence already, and Natalie's in custody and talking." Gray didn't know if this were true, but neither would Cameron. He didn't respond, though. "You're in deep shit, Cameron. Killing your brother, framing your father."

"This is bullshit."

Gray read Cameron his rights.

Fifty One

McGavin's restaurant was full, but the man himself was nowhere in sight. A waiter pointed Gray towards the kitchen where McGavin was looking over the menu for the day.

"Ah, Sergeant Gray, come to take me up on my offer?"

"Just the opposite, McGavin. Your offer is refused."

"I'm confused. What are you wittering on about?"

"I got a text earlier, from a friendly solicitor. Cameron was selling EAP over to Millstone in its entirety. For an excellent price. For you. We're talking past tense though now. I thought you should hear from me first that Cameron has been arrested. The deal's off."

"I've already told you, Millstone is nothing to do with me."

"Everything is down to you. Your fingermarks are all over it. I know you had Noble murdered."

"Perhaps you should give up your job and write a book. Fiction, of course, because that's what this is."

"Not before I've put you away."

"You have *nothing*. Otherwise you'd have the cuffs on already." McGavin forced another smile.

"One day, McGavin. One day soon."

"I look forward to it, Sergeant. Now, get out of my restaurant."

Fifty Two

The room was a rectangle. On one side was an examination table, and in the opposite corner Doctor Kahn's desk faced the wall.

Gray settled into one of two seats next to the desk. Kahn – a thirty-something Asian woman already turning grey, with small, serious features– twisted in her seat to face him. The surgery was one of those where you could end up seeing any of the GPs. Gone were the days of being allocated a single physician who you saw forever more.

Kahn started with the standard question. "What prompted you to come see me?"

"I've been sick several times. Most recently there was blood."

Kahn made a note on her pad. "Any other symptoms?"

"I've been finding it hard to swallow when eating. Also heartburn."

"How long for now?"

"Three, maybe four weeks."

"Is there anything which makes your symptoms better or worse?"

Gray considered that. "I don't know. I haven't really thought about it. Milk helps ease the heartburn, but otherwise I assumed it was bad food or irritable bowel syndrome."

"Do you smoke?"

"Some, I've been cutting back."

"Drink alcohol?"

"Same answer."

"How recently have you been reducing your intake?"

"A few months now, which is why I thought this was linked to a lifestyle change."

"Okay, I'd like to take some blood, then examine you."

"I hate needles," said Gray.

"It's necessary, I'm afraid."

Reluctantly, Gray agreed.

"Would you prefer to lie down?" asked Kahn.

"Yes."

He shrugged off his jacket, rolled up his right sleeve, and lay on the examination table. As Kahn tightened a strap around his upper arm just above the elbow, Gray twisted his head away and covered up his eyes with his left arm as if he were a weeping angel. Kahn tapped on a vein.

"You'll feel a sharp scratch," she said.

This time Gray kept his comments to himself. Without further warning the needle pushed through his skin and then the vein. Gray grimaced and sucked in half a lungful of air through his teeth.

"Thank you, Mr Gray. Just stay there a moment please."

Gray did as he was told while Kahn returned to her desk and tapped at her computer. When she'd finished she turned to face him. "I'm going to urgently refer you to a specialist at the hospital for an endoscopy. The symptoms you're displaying concern me sufficiently – weight loss, the reflux, the difficulty in swallowing – and the period of time you've been suffering for. By then we should have the bloods back."

"What do you think it could be?"

"Any number of causes are possible."

Gray considered what the doctor was saying. "It's cancer, right?"

"Not necessarily. At this stage I'd really try not to worry. Your symptoms could equally be due to Barrett's oesophagus, where the cells around the oesophagus are weakened. Or any number of other things. My referral is a precautionary measure. Any further questions?"

"I can't think of any right now."

At reception, Gray gave them his mobile number, then he was outside and wondering what the hell he could do, other than go home.

GRAY OPENED UP THE floor-to-ceiling windows to let in some air into his flat. He stood staring out over the water for a few minutes, seeing nothing. In the two days since Cameron and Natalie's arrest the case had changed completely. The charges over the Sunset fire against Jake had been dropped, and he'd been released, but Hamson was gathering evidence regarding Regan's alleged sexual assaults, and Jake's possible collusion in a series of cover-ups.

Cameron had been charged with murder, but was remaining silent. Natalie's charge was accessory to murder. Gray had heard from Fowler that she was co-operating fully with his colleagues. It seemed her motive had simply been to destroy Jake, to publicly tear his life apart, raze everything he'd built to the ground.

The murder of William Noble remained open. Privately, the police believed he'd died at the hands of McGavin because Noble was digging into Millstone, but without the evidence it was another unsolved.

Right now, Gray felt as low as was possible. He was coming to accept Carslake had lied to him and probably had for years. Though it was tough to accept. Hamson had been right all along, but their friendship was broken, perhaps beyond repair.

This morning Gray had received an email from Inspector Morel in Calais. He couldn't find any record of a child with Tom's description coming through the port. The Dover witness probably never existed in the first place. Gray had to accept it was all a subterfuge from Carslake to put him off. But why?

Gray decided to have a beer. If he had cancer, then what the hell. His mobile rang as he was reaching for a bottle. "Hello, Rachel." He was surprised to hear from her.

"Afternoon, Sergeant Gray." She sounded tired.

"Sol, please. How are you?"

"Worn out, but I feel brilliant. I don't really have anyone else to tell so I rang you, I hope that's all right. My baby arrived last night."

"Congratulations!" Gray was genuinely pleased for her. "Boy or girl?"

"A little boy. I've decided I'm going to call him Thomas."

Gray's heart lurched, but it could only be coincidence. Gray had never discussed his private life with her. "Good choice, I'll come see you later, okay?"

"I'd like that." Gray heard Thomas cry in the background. "I've got to go, Sol. He's a hungry one."

BURN THE EVIDENCE

Holding his mobile, Gray realised a massive error of judgement. All these years he'd been chasing the past, seeking the missing, pining for the dead, when there was someone here who'd needed him. Someone Gray had abandoned, like Natalie had abandoned Rachel. He'd been a fool and worse. But at least he could try to undo his errors.

Gray pulled out his laptop. He entered Facebook Messenger, typed out his daughter's name, and wrote her a note. A moment later a speech bubble and three bouncing dots appeared.

She was typing.

Her reply seemed to take forever, but when they appeared the words sent Gray's heart soaring. "Hi Dad, I've missed you."

Despite everything, maybe there was a future after all.

Fifty Three

Jeff Carslake's mobile rang. His spare, the pay-as-you-go, the one only a handful of people had the number to. He stared at the number, not recognising it. A landline. But it had to be somebody Carslake knew. He didn't trust giving his details to just anyone.

"Hello?"

"Hello, yourself."

"Who is this?" asked Carslake. The voice was familiar, the memory distant.

"You mean after all this time you've forgotten me? Now that's just plain rude."

The caller's tone was playful, amused.

"It's been a long day."

"Well, we can make our acquaintance again soon, Chief Inspector Carslake, because I'll be getting out."

"Out?"

"From where you put me. This time you can't stop it happening. The wheels of justice are in motion. Slowly, mind, so it'll be a few months before we shake hands again. I just thought you'd like to know."

A memory was stirring within Carslake. "Duncan?"

"The one and only Duncan Usher. I knew you wouldn't let me down. Well, not again anyway."

"You're being released?"

"That's what I said. I'll be coming home. First person I'll be having a word with is Solomon Gray. He'll be very interested in what I have to say."

"What about?" asked Carslake, though he already knew the answer.

"His lad, Tom, of course. I'll be seeing you soon, Jeff. And it's not going to be pretty. Count on it."

Carslake cut the call. He threw the phone on his desk. He'd be getting rid of it, now it was compromised. Carslake was taken aback. Duncan Usher was getting out of prison, and he hadn't had a clue. He and Usher agreed on one point.

It wasn't going to be pretty.

If you enjoyed Burn The Evidence I'd greatly appreciate it if you would write a review. They really help authors like me grow and develop.

Thanks! It means a great deal to me.

And if you want to sign up to a periodic newsletter with information on launches, special offers etc. (no spam!) then you can do so HERE[1].

---

1. https://mailchi.mp/4bbaf7efe867/keith-nixon-free-book

In return is a free book in the Konstantin series, Russian Roulette, a unique and gritty crime thriller featuring an ex-KGB operative living undercover in Margate.

Other Novels by Keith Nixon

The Solomon Gray Series
 Dig Two Graves
Burn The Evidence
Beg For Mercy
Bury The Bodies
The Konstantin Series
Russian Roulette
The Fix
I'm Dead Again
Dark Heart, Heavy Soul
The DI Granger Series
The Corpse Role
The Caradoc Series
The Eagle's Shadow
The Eagle's Blood

About the Author

Keith Nixon is a British born writer of crime and historical fiction novels. Originally, he trained as a chemist, but Keith is now in a senior sales role for a high-tech business. Keith currently lives with his family in the North West of England.

Readers can connect with Keith on various social media platforms:

Web: http://www.keithnixon.co.uk
Twitter: @knntom[1]
Facebook: Keithnixonauthor[2]
Blog: www.keithnixon.co.uk/blog[3]

---

1. https://twitter.com/knntom
2. https://www.facebook.com/keithnixonauthor/
3. http://www.keithnixon.co.uk/blog

Burn The Evidence
Published by Gladius Press 2018
Copyright © Keith Nixon 2018
Second Edition

Keith Nixon has asserted his right under the Copyright, Designs and Patents Act 1998 to be identified as the author of this work

CONDITIONS OF SALE

All rights reserved. No part of this publication may be reproduced, stored in a retrieval system, or transmitted in any form or by any means, electronic, mechanical, photocopying, scanning, recording or otherwise, without the prior permission of the publisher

This book has been sold subject to the condition that it shall not, by way of trade or otherwise, be lent, resold, hired out, or otherwise circulated without the publisher's prior consent in any form of binding or cover other than that in which it is published and without a similar condition including this condition being imposed on the subsequent purchaser.

All characters in this publication are fictitious and any resemblance to real persons, living or dead is purely coincidental.

Cover design by Jim Divine.

Don't miss out!

Visit the website below and you can sign up to receive emails whenever Keith Nixon publishes a new book. There's no charge and no obligation.

https://books2read.com/r/B-A-BGNH-UBXW

BOOKS 2 READ

Connecting independent readers to independent writers.

Did you love *Burn The Evidence*? Then you should read *Beg For Mercy* by Keith Nixon!

Two men fight to prove their innocence. A cop and a convicted murderer. One of them is lying. Fifteen years ago, local crime boss Duncan Usher was sent to prison for killing his wife. A young Detective Solomon Gray was first at the scene and instrumental in putting Usher away. But now Usher is out, released on a technicality.Usher has held a grudge all this time, and he won't stop until he gets revenge on the dirty cop who framed him all those years ago. Usher wants Gray's help, acting as an inside man within the police. Gray refuses, but Usher has leverage – information on Gray's missing son. Gray agrees to work with Usher because he'll do anything to find his son.

But Gray is taking a huge risk; playing both sides of the game and carrying out his own investigation into what really happened fifteen years ago.**Can Gray get to the truth? Or will the past bring Gray down?**Set in the once grand town of Margate in the south of England, the now broken and depressed seaside resort becomes its own character in this dark detective thriller, perfect for fans of Ian Rankin, Stuart MacBride, and Peter James.Beg For Mercy is the third book in the series featuring Detective Sergeant Solomon Gray. Buy it now to discover whether Gray can track down the real killer and escape Usher's clutches in this tense crime series.

What Others Say

"Nixon combines his trademark gritty humour with a flawless police procedural."**M.W. Craven**, author of the *Washington Poe* series"A compelling murder mystery with a multilayered and engaging new hero. Great read."**Mason Cross**, author of the *Carter Blake* thriller series"A dark, uncompromising tale of loss, murder, and revenge. Glorious noir, which takes the police procedural elements and gives them new life. I can't wait to read the next step in Solomon Gray's journey for answers ..."**Luca Veste**, author of the *Murphy and Rossi* crime series"Be prepared for everything to resolve in dramatic fashion."**Crime Fiction Lover**

What Readers Say

"I follow a lot of Detective series but this is by far one of the best.""You've no idea how glad I am to be back in Gray's world!""The author has such an amazing talent for telling tales.""Hard to put down and gripping to the very end.""There has to be another installment soon!""Wow, this series just gets better.""Another strong instalment in a thoroughly enjoyable series.""A fantastic read with brilliant characters.""A very entertaining and well executed thriller. ""... deeply emotional, a dark rollercoaster ride."**Ed James**, author of bestselling *DI Fenchurch* series

Also by Keith Nixon

Caradoc
The Eagle's Shadow

Detective Solomon Gray
Dig Two Graves
Burn The Evidence
Beg For Mercy
Bury The Bodies

DI Granger
The Corpse Role

Konstantin
Russian Roulette
The Fix
I'm Dead Again

Dark Heart, Heavy Soul

Standalone
The Solomon Gray Series: Books 1 to 4: Gripping Police Thrillers With A Difference

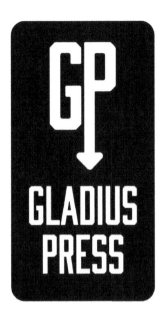

About the Publisher

Gladius Press is a small, yet highly innovative publisher of crime, humour and historical fiction novels based in Manchester in the UK.

Printed in Great Britain
by Amazon